God *and* Jesus

Exploring The Biblical Distinction

Joel W. Hemphill

Trumpet Call Books

P.O. Box 656

Joelton, Tennessee 37080

Trumpet Call Books

P.O. Box 656
Joelton, TN 37080

www.thehemphills.com • www.trumpetcallbooks.com

God and Jesus

ISBN: 978-0-9825196-5-3

Printed in the United States of America

Photos of Joel and LaBreeska Hemphill by
Bloodworth Photography – Goodlettsville, TN.

Table of Contents

Thanks To… 5

Dedication 7

Introduction.. 9

Matthew 13

Mark 23

Luke 31

John... 47

Acts 67

Romans 75

First Corinthians.. 81

Second Corinthians 85

Galatians 89

Ephesians 93

Philippians.. 99

Colossians 101

Hebrews 119

James... 125

First Peter 127

Second Peter.. 131

First John.. 133

Second John 137

Jude 139

Revelation 141

Jesus Is Our Brother.. 189

What About John One?... 199

Checking Our Doctrine And Worship 243

Learning About God From Jesus 271

A Unique Sinless Man 275

We Believe.....

*"At that time **Christ** will destroy all rulers, authorities, and powers, and he will hand over the kingdom to **God** the Father. Christ must rule until he puts all enemies under his control. The last enemy to be destroyed will be death. The Scripture says that God put all things under his [Jesus'] control. When it says "all things" are under him, it is clear this does not include God himself. God is the One who put everything under his control. <u>After everything has been put under the **Son**, then **he**</u> [Jesus] <u>**will put himself under God**</u>, who had put all things under him. <u>**Then God will be the complete ruler over everything**</u>"* (*1 Corinthians 15:24-28* Thomas Nelson's *New Century Version*).*

*Read it in your favorite version-it says the same!

Thanks To...

LaBreeska, my darling wife of fifty-six years for your love for this truth and your willingness to sacrifice to proclaim it. Great is your reward!

Our dedicated secretary Dawn Mansfield who tirelessly typed and re-typed the manuscript, and in whom I can trust for helpful advice.

Dr. Joe Martin for your friendship and for pointing out to me that there are so many verses that make the distinction that is the focus of this book.

Our dear friends Dan and Sharon Gill of Twenty-first Century Reformation, www.21stcr.org, for your encouragement, and being willing to "spend and be spent" to take this biblical message to the world.

Two sweet and talented ladies, Nancy Carter of Quality DigiPress for your skillful interior design, and Lynsae Harkins of Lynsae Printing and Design for the expert cover artwork and design.

All who love truth more than tradition and "thus says the word of God" more than the doctrines of men.

God's richest blessings to all of the above through Christ Jesus our Savior!

Dedication

This book is dedicated to those who have seen this awesome truth and then had the courage to speak out. I honor you! Benjamin Franklin said, *"As we must account for every idle word, so must we account for every idle silence."*

God The Creator's Glory

*"Thus saith the Lord, the Holy **One** of Israel, and his Maker. **I have made the earth**, and **created man** upon it: I, even **my hands**, have stretched out the heavens, and all their host have I commanded....and there is **no God else beside me**; a just God and a Saviour; **there is none beside me.** Look unto me, and be ye saved, all the ends of the earth: **for I am God, and there is none else"** (Isaiah 45:11-12, 21-22).*

*"I am the Lord: that is my name; and **my glory will I not give to another"** (Isaiah 42:8).*

"I will not give my glory unto another" *(Isaiah 48:11).*

*"And I saw another angel fly in the midst of heaven, having the everlasting gospel to preach unto them that dwell on the earth...Saying with a loud voice, **Fear God**, and **give glory to him**; for the hour of his judgement is come: and **worship him** that made heaven, and the earth, and the sea, and the fountains of waters"* *(Revelation 14:6-7).*

Jesus' Glory

*"....and we beheld **his glory**, the glory as of **the only begotten of the Father**" (John 1:14).*

*"The Son of Man...shall come in **his own glory"** [Jesus speaking] (Luke 9:26).*

*"The Son of man shall sit in the throne of **his glory**"* [Jesus speaking] *(Matt. 19:28).*

*"Father...the **glory which thou gavest me**...that they may behold **my glory which thou hast given me"** [Jesus speaking] (John 17:21, 22, 24).*

[Christ] *"verily was **foreordained** before the foundation of the world, but was manifest in these last times for you, Who by him do believe in **God**, that raised him up from the dead, and **gave him glory**; that your faith and hope might be in **God"** (I Peter 1:20-21).*

Introduction

It is a sad truth of our time that Christianity mostly teaches and worships Jesus to the exclusion of God our Father. Listen to the sermons and the songs! Even many of those who direct their prayers to the Father seem unclear as to whom they are speaking. (Note: The Father did not die for our sins since He is *"immortal,"* which means, incapable of dying).

Somehow we have merged Jesus and God in our thinking. This is a serious error because to picture God as only six feet tall is to lose our healthy, reverential fear of Him. Even more serious is our tendency to rob God the Father of the glory of who He alone is, and what He alone has done, and give it to His awesome Son, our Savior Jesus Messiah. Consider this:

> *"...the beginning of the creation which **God** created"* [Jesus speaking] *(Mark 13:19).*

> *"For **God** so loved the world, that he gave..."* *(John 3:16).*

> *"Behold, what manner of love the **Father** hath bestowed on us..."* *(I John 3:1).*

> *"**God** that made the world and all things therein, seeing that he is Lord of heaven and earth...And hath made of one blood all nations of men for to*

dwell on all the face of the earth...And the times of this ignorance God winked at; but now commandeth all men every where to repent: Because he [God] *hath appointed a day, in the which he* [God] *will judge the world in righteousness by that man* [Jesus] *whom he* [God] *hath ordained; whereof he* [God] *hath given assurance unto all men, in that he* [God] *hath raised him* [Jesus] *from the dead"* [Paul preaching on Mars' hill] (Acts 17:24, 26, 30, 31). Question--Do you know *"God"*, or only *"that man"*?

Jesus came to show us God our Father. He was his favorite subject, and according to the N.T. he mentioned the Father some one hundred-seventy times. This is far more than he spoke of heaven, hell, money, marriage, divorce, or any other subject! Yes, Jesus wants us *to see the Father through himself,* but it is for sure that Jesus never intended that we *lose the Father in himself,* as we have done! The purpose of this book is to help correct this error.

There are over 760 N.T. passages that make a clear distinction between God and Jesus. Most do not specify *"God the Father,"* because in the doctrine of the N.T. the Father **is** *"the only true God" (John 17:3; I Cor. 8:6; Eph. 1:3, 4:6; I Peter 1:3; etc.).* Sixty-two times the N.T. says *"God **and** Jesus"* (or *"Christ,"* or *"the Lamb"*). In each of these the word *"and"* is the Greek word *"kai,"* and it means *"also"* or *"in addition to."* For example when the Bible says in Acts 3:1 that *"Peter **and** John"* went up into the temple to pray, are we expected to believe that Peter *"is"* John? Of course not! It is telling us of **two** separate and distinct persons

10

who went up to the temple, Peter **in addition to**, John. Likewise, when the Bible says in John 11:19 that many of the Jews came to comfort *"Martha **and** Mary"* concerning the death of their brother, are we being led to believe that Martha *"is"* Mary? No way! It is telling us that Lazarus had two sisters, Martha **in addition to** Mary! So why in the name of all sound reasoning do we read the following verses, and many more similar ones, as if they say, **God is Jesus (or, Jesus is God)?**

> *"...the only true **God**, **and** **Jesus** Christ, whom thou hast sent" (John 17:3).*

> [Stephen] *"...saw the glory of **God**, **and** **Jesus** standing on the right hand of **God**" (Acts 7:55).*

> *"...peace from **God** our Father, **and** the Lord **Jesus** Christ" (Romans 1:7).*

> *"But to us there is but one **God**...**and** one Lord **Jesus**" (I Cor. 8:6).*

> *"Paul, and apostle...by **Jesus** Christ, **and** **God** the Father" (Gal. 1:1).*

> *"Peace...from **God** the Father **and** the Lord **Jesus** Christ" (Eph. 6:23).*

> *"Now our Lord **Jesus** Christ himself, **and** **God**, even our Father" (II Thess. 2:16).*

11

*"For there is one **God**, and one mediator...**Jesus**" (I Tim. 2:5).*

*"But ye are come...to **God**...and to **Jesus**" (Heb. 12:22-24).*

*"...the knowledge of **God**, and of **Jesus**" (II Peter 1:2).*

*"...denying the only Lord **God**, and our Lord **Jesus**" (Jude 1:4).*

*"...the kingdom of our **God**, and his **Christ**" (Rev. 12:10).*

Precious friend, there are fifty more such verses. For instance, the apostle Paul wrote thirteen books in the N.T. and he introduces each one with this greeting, *"Grace to you and peace from **God**...**and Jesus**"* (no third person is mentioned). Again, there are over 760 passages that distinguish the two!

Verses that distinguish God from Jesus.

Chapter 1

Matthew

*T*he gospel of Matthew contains sixty-nine passages that make a clear distinction between God and Jesus. They are:

2:11-12   "And when they were come into the house, they saw the **young child** [Jesus] with Mary his mother...And being warned of **God** in a dream that they should not return to Herod, they departed into their own country another way."

2:13   "And when they were departed, behold, the angel of the **Lord** [God] appeareth to Joseph in a dream, saying, Arise, and take the **young child** and his mother, and flee into Egypt...."

2:15   "And was there until the death of Herod: that it might be fulfilled which was spoken of the **Lord** [God] by the prophet, saying, Out of Egypt have I called **my son** [Jesus]."

2:19-20   "...an angel of the **Lord** [God] appeareth in a dream to Joseph in Egypt, Saying, Arise, and take the **young child** and his mother, and go into the land of Israel... ."

2:21-22   "And he arose, and took the **young child** and his mother, and came into the land of Israel...

13

notwithstanding, being warned of God in a dream, he turned aside into the parts of Galilee... ."

3:16   "And Jesus, when he was baptized...the heavens were opened unto him, and he saw the Spirit of God descending like a dove, and lighting upon him... ."

3:17   "And lo a voice from heaven [God], saying, This is my Beloved Son [Jesus], in whom I am well-pleased."

4:4   "But he [Jesus] answered and said, It is written, Man shall not live by bread alone, but by every word that proceedeth out of the mouth of God."

4:7   "Jesus said unto him, It is written again, Thou shalt not tempt [i.e. put to the test] the Lord thy God." Note: The devil had tempted Jesus to cast himself down from the pinnacle of the temple and see if God would save him. This was Jesus' response.

4:10   "Then saith Jesus unto him, Thou shalt worship the Lord thy God, and him only shalt thou serve."

5:2,8   "And he [Jesus] opened his mouth, and taught them, saying...Blessed are the pure in heart: for they shall see God."

5:34   "But I [Jesus] say unto you, Swear not at all; neither by heaven; for it is God's throne."

6:5-6   "...Verily **I** [Jesus] say unto you...pray to thy **Father** which is in secret; and thy Father which seeth in secret shall reward thee openly."

6-16-18   "...Verily **I** [Jesus] say unto you, They have their reward. But thou, when thou fastest, anoint thine head, and wash thy face; That thou appear not unto men to fast, but unto thy **Father** which is in secret... ."

6:24-25   "Ye cannot serve **God** and mammon.   Therefore **I** [Jesus] say unto you, Take no thought for your life... ."

7:24   "Not every one that saith unto **me** [Jesus], Lord, Lord, shall enter into the kingdom of heaven; but he that doeth the will of my **Father** which is in heaven."

9:6,8   "But that ye may know that the **Son of man** hath power on earth to forgive sins, (then saith he to the sick of the palsy,) Arise, take up thy bed, and go unto thine house... But when the multitudes saw it, they marvelled, and glorified **God**, which had given such power unto men."

9:37-38   Then saith **he** [Jesus] unto his disciples... Pray ye therefore the **Lord of the harvest** [God], that he will send forth labourers into his harvest."

10:27-28   "What **I** [Jesus] tell you in darkness, that speak ye in light... fear **him** [God] which is able to destroy both soul and body in hell."

10:32   "Whosoever therefore shall confess **me** [Jesus] before men, him will I confess also before my **Father** which is in heaven."

10:33   "But whosoever shall deny **me** [Jesus] before men, him will I also deny before my **Father** which is in heaven."

11:25   "...**Jesus** answered and said, I thank thee, O **Father**, Lord of heaven and earth, because thou hast hid these things... Even so, Father: for so it seemed good in thy sight."

11:27   "All things are delivered unto **me** [Jesus] of my **Father**... ."

12:3-4   "But **he** [Jesus] said unto them, Have ye not read what David did, when he was an hungred... How he entered into the house of **God**, and did eat the shewbread... ."

12:18   "Behold **my servant** [Jesus], whom **I** [God] have chosen; my beloved, in whom my soul is well pleased: I will put my spirit upon him... ."

12:28   "But if **I** [Jesus] cast out devils by the Spirit of **God**, then the kingdom of God is come unto you."

12:32   "And whosoever speaketh a word against the **Son of man**, it shall be forgiven him: but whosoever speaketh against the **Holy Ghost** [the Spirit of God],it shall not be forgiven him... ."

12:50   "For whosoever shall do the will of **my** [Jesus'] **Father** which is in heaven, the same is my brother, and sister, and mother."

14:33   "...Of a truth **thou** [Jesus] art the Son of **God**."

15:3,4   "But **he** [Jesus] answered and said unto them, Why do ye also transgress the commandment of **God** by your tradition? For God commanded, saying... ."

15:13   "But **he** [Jesus] answered and said, Every plant, which my heavenly **Father** hath not planted, shall be rooted up ."

15:30-31   "And great multitudes came unto him, having with them those that were lame, blind, dumb, maimed, and many others, and cast them down at Jesus' feet; and he healed them...and they glorified the **God** of Israel."

16:15-16   "**He** [Jesus] saith unto them, But whom say ye that I am? And Simon Peter answered and said, Thou art the Christ, the Son of the living **God**."

16:17   "And **Jesus** answered and said unto him, Blessed art thou, Simon Bar–jona: for flesh and blood hath not revealed it unto thee, but my **Father** which is in heaven."

16:23   "But **he** [Jesus] turned, and said unto Peter... thou savourest not the things that be of **God**, but those that be of men."

16:27   "For the **Son of man** shall come in the glory of his **Father** with his angels... ."

17:5   "...and behold **a voice** [God] out of the cloud, which said, This is my **beloved Son**, in whom I am well pleased; hear ye him."

18:10   "...**I** [Jesus] say unto you, That in heaven their angels do always behold the face of my **Father** which is in heaven."

18:11,14   "For the **Son of man** is come to save that which was lost. Even so it is not the will of your **Father** which is in heaven, that one of these little ones should perish."

18:19   "Again **I** [Jesus] say unto you, That if two of you shall agree on earth as touching any thing that they shall ask, it shall be done for them of my **Father** which is in heaven."

18:35   "So likewise shall **my** [Jesus'] heavenly **Father** do also unto you, if ye from your hearts forgive not every one his brother their trespasses."

19:4   "And **he** [Jesus] answered and said unto them, Have ye not read, that **he** [God] which made them at the beginning made them male and female... ."

19:17   "And **he** [Jesus] said unto him, Why callest thou me good? there is none good but one, that is, **God**... ."

19:24   "And again **I** [Jesus] say unto you, It is easier for a camel to go through the eye of a needle, than for a rich man to enter into the kingdom of **God**."

19:26   "But **Jesus** beheld them, and said unto them, With men this is impossible; but with **God** all things are possible."

20:23   "And **he** [Jesus] saith unto them...to sit on my right hand, and on my left, is not mine to give, but it shall be given to them for whom it is prepared of my **Father**."

21:9   "...Blessed is **he** [Jesus] that cometh in the name of the **Lord** [God]... ."

21:12   "And **Jesus** went into the temple of **God**, and cast out all them that sold and bought in the temple... ."

21:31   "...**Jesus** saith unto them, Verily I say unto you, That the publicans and the harlots go into the kingdom of **God** before you."

21:37   "But last of all **he** [God] sent unto them his **son** [Jesus], saying, They will reverence my son."

21:39-40   "And they caught **him** [the son-Jesus], and cast him out of the vineyard, and slew him. When **the lord of the vineyard** [God the Father] cometh, what will he do unto those husbandmen?"

21:42   "**Jesus** saith unto them...The stone which the builders rejected, the same is become the head of the corner: this is the **Lord's** [God's] doing... ."

21:43   "Therefore say **I** [Jesus] unto you, The kingdom of **God** shall be taken from you, and given to a nation bringing forth the fruits thereof."

22:16   "...Master, we know that **thou** [Jesus] art true, and teachest the way of **God** in truth... ."

22:21   "...Then saith **he** [Jesus] unto them, Render therefore unto Caesar the things which are Caesar's; and unto **God** the things that are God's."

22:29   "**Jesus** answered and said unto them, Ye do err, not knowing the scriptures, nor the power of **God**."

22:37   "**Jesus** said unto him, Thou shalt love the Lord thy **God** with all thy heart... ."

22:43-44   "**He** [Jesus] saith unto them, How then doth David in spirit call him Lord, saying, The **Lord** [God] said unto my **Lord** [Jesus], Sit thou on my right hand, till I make thine enemies thy footstool?"

23:9-10   "And call no man your father upon the earth: for one is your **Father**, which is in heaven. Neither be ye called masters: for one is your Master, even **Christ**."

23:39   "For I say unto you, Ye shall not see **me** [Jesus] henceforth, till ye shall say, Blessed is he that cometh in the name of the **Lord** [God]."

24:34,36   "Verily **I** [Jesus] say unto you... of that day and hour knoweth no man, no, not the angels of heaven, but my **Father** only."

25:34   "Then shall the **King** [Jesus] say unto them on His right hand, Come, ye blessed of my **Father**... ."

26:29   "...I [Jesus] will not drink henceforth of this fruit of the vine, until that day when I drink it new with you in my **Father's** kingdom."

26:39   "...O my **Father**, if it be possible, let this cup pass from **me** [Jesus]: nevertheless not as I will, but as thou wilt."

26:42   "**He** [Jesus] went away again the second time, and prayed, saying, O my **Father**, if this cup may not pass away from me, except I drink it, thy will be done."

26:53   "Thinkest thou that **I** [Jesus] cannot now pray to my **Father**, and he shall presently give me more than twelve legions of angels?"

26:64   "**Jesus** saith unto him...Hereafter shall ye see the Son of man sitting on the **right hand of power** [God], and coming in the clouds of heaven."

27:46   "And about the ninth hour **Jesus** cried with a loud voice, saying...**My God, my God**, why hast thou forsaken me?"

27:54   "...Truly this was the **Son** [Jesus] of **God**."

Chapter 2

Mark

*T*he gospel of Mark contains forty-five passages that make a clear distinction between God and Jesus. They are:

1:1   "The beginning of the gospel of **Jesus** Christ, the Son of **God**... ."

1:2   "...Behold, **I** [God] send my messenger before **thy** [Jesus] face, which shall prepare thy way before thee."

1:11-12   "And there came a voice from heaven, saying, Thou art **my** [God's] beloved **Son**, in whom I am well pleased. And immediately the Spirit driveth him into the wilderness."

1:14   "...**Jesus** came into Galilee, preaching the gospel of the kingdom of **God**... ."

2:11-12   "**I** [Jesus] say unto thee, Arise...And immediately he arose, took up the bed, and went forth before them all; insomuch that they were all amazed, and glorified **God**... ."

2:25-26   "And **he** [Jesus] said unto them, Have ye never read what David did...How he went into the house of **God**...and did eat the shewbread... ."

3:34-35   "And **he** [Jesus] looked round about on them which sat about him, and said...whosoever shall do the will of **God**, the same is my brother, and my sister, and mother."

4:11   "And **he** [Jesus] said unto them, Unto you it is given to know the mystery of the kingdom of **God**... ."

4:26   "And **he** [Jesus] said, So is the kingdom of **God**, as if a man should cast seed into the ground... ."

4:30   "And **he** [Jesus] said, Whereunto shall we liken the kingdom of **God**?"

7:6,8   "**He** [Jesus] answered and said unto them...laying aside the commandment of **God**, ye hold the tradition of men... ."

7:9   "And **he** [Jesus] said unto them, Full well ye reject the commandment of **God**, that ye may keep your own tradition."

8:33   "But when **he** [Jesus] had turned about and looked on his disciples, he rebuked Peter, saying...thou savourest not the things that be of **God**, but the things that be of men."

8:38   "Whosoever therefore shall be ashamed of **me** [Jesus]...of him also shall the Son of man be ashamed, when he cometh in the glory of his **Father** with the holy angels."

9:1   "And **he** [Jesus] said unto them...there be some of them that stand here, which shall not taste of death, till they have seen the kingdom of **God** come with power."

9:7   "...and a **voice** [God] came out of the cloud, saying, This is my beloved **Son**: hear him."

9:37   "Whosoever...shall receive me receiveth not **me**, [Jesus] but **him** [God] that sent me."

10:5-6   "And **Jesus** answered and said unto them...from the beginning of the creation **God** made them male and female."

10:9-10   "What therefore **God** hath joined together, let not man put asunder. And in the house his disciples asked **him** [Jesus] again of the same matter."

10:14   "But when **Jesus** saw it, he was much displeased, and said unto them...of such is the kingdom of **God**."

10:15   "Verily **I** [Jesus] say unto you, Whosoever shall not receive the kingdom of **God** as a little child, he shall not enter therein."

10:18   "And **Jesus** said unto him, Why callest thou me good? there is none good but one, that is, **God**."

10:23   "And **Jesus** looked round about, and saith unto his disciples, How hardly shall they that have riches enter into the kingdom of **God**!"

10:24   "...But **Jesus** answereth again, and saith unto them, Children, how hard is it for them that trust in riches to enter into the kingdom of **God**!"

10:27   "And **Jesus** looking upon them saith, With men it is impossible, but not with **God**: for with **God** all things are possible."

11:9   "...Blessed is **he** [Jesus] that cometh in the name of the **Lord** [God]."

11:17   "And **he** [Jesus] taught, saying unto them, Is it not written, **My** [God's] house shall be called of all nations the house of prayer?"

11:22   "And **Jesus** answering saith unto them, Have faith in **God**."

11:24-25   "Therefore **I** [Jesus] say unto you...forgive, if ye have ought against any: that your **Father** also which is in heaven may forgive you your trespasses."

12:6   "Having yet therefore one **son** [Jesus], his wellbeloved, **he** [God] sent him also last unto them, saying, They will reverence my son."

12:14   "...**Master** [Jesus], we know that thou art true, and...teachest the way of **God** in truth: Is it lawful to give tribute to Caesar, or not?"

12:17   "And **Jesus** answering said unto them, Render to Caesar the things that are Caesar's, and to **God** the things that are God's."

12:24,26   "And **Jesus** answering said unto them, Do ye not therefore err, because ye know not the scriptures, neither the power of **God**?" And as touching the dead, that they rise: have ye not read in the book of Moses, how in the bush **God** spake unto him... ."

12:29-30   "And **Jesus** answered him, The first of all the commandments is, Hear, O Israel; The Lord our **God** is one Lord: And thou shalt love the Lord thy **God** with all thy heart... ."

12:32   "... Well, **Master** [Jesus], thou hast said the truth: for there is one **God**; and there is none other but he... ."

12:34   "And when **Jesus** saw that he answered discreetly, he said unto him, Thou art not far from the kingdom of **God**."

12:35-36   "And Jesus answered and said... David himself said by the Holy Ghost, The **Lord** [God] said to my **Lord** [Messiah-Jesus], Sit thou on my right hand, till I make thine enemies thy footstool."

13:5,19   "And **Jesus** answering them began to say...For in those days shall be affliction, such as was not from the beginning of the creation which **God** created... ."

13:32   "But of that day and that hour knoweth no man, no, not the angels which are in heaven, neither the **Son**, but the **Father**."

14:25   "Verily I say unto you, I will drink no more of the fruit of the vine, until that day that **I** [Jesus] drink it new in the kingdom of **God**."

14:36   "And **he** [Jesus] said, Abba, **Father**, all things are possible unto thee; take away this cup from me: nevertheless not what I will, but what thou wilt."

14:61   "...Art thou the Christ, the Son of the **Blessed** [God]? And **Jesus** said, I am... ."

15:34   "And at the ninth hour **Jesus** cried with a loud voice, saying...My **God**, my **God**, why hast thou forsaken me?"

15:43   "Joseph of Arimathaea...which also waited for the kingdom of **God**, came, and went in boldly unto Pilate, and craved the body of **Jesus**."

16:19   "So then after the **Lord** [Jesus] had spoken unto them, he was received up into heaven, and sat on the right hand of **God**."

> *"A simple man with the Scripture has more authority than the Pope or a council."*
>
> **Christian Reformer Martin Luther**

Chapter 3

Luke

*T*he gospel of Luke contains ninety-nine passages that make a clear distinction between God and Jesus. They are:

1:31-32   "...and shalt call his name **Jesus**. He shall be great, and shall be called the Son of the Highest; and the **Lord God** shall give unto him the throne of his father David."

1:35   "And the angel answered and said unto her, The Holy Ghost shall come upon thee, and the power of the **Highest** [God] shall overshadow thee: therefore also that holy thing which shall be born of thee shall be called the **Son** of God."

2:12-14   "...Ye shall find the **babe** [Jesus] wrapped in swaddling clothes, lying in a manger. And suddenly there was with the angel a multitude of the heavenly host praising **God**, and saying, Glory to God in the highest, and on earth peace... ."

2:15-16   "...Let us now go even unto Bethlehem, and see this thing which is come to pass, which the **Lord** [God] hath made known unto us. And they came with haste, and found Mary, and Joseph, and the **babe** [Jesus] lying in a manger."

2:17,20   "And when they had seen it, they made known abroad the saying which was told them concerning this **child** [Jesus]. And the shepherds returned, glorifying and praising **God** for all the things that they had heard and seen, as it was told unto them."

2:22   "And when the days of her purification according to the law of Moses were accomplished, they brought **him** [Jesus] to Jerusalem, to present him to the **Lord** [God]... ."

2:26   "And it was revealed unto him [Simeon] by the Holy Ghost, that he should not see death, before he had seen the **Lord's** [God's] **Christ** [Messiah]."

2:27-28   "... and when the parents brought in the child **Jesus**...[Simeon] took he him up in his arms, and blessed **God**... ."

2:29-30   "**Lord** [God], now let thy servant depart in peace, according to thy word: For mine eyes have seen **thy salvation** [Jesus], Which thou hast prepared... ."

2:38   "And she coming in that instant gave thanks likewise unto The **Lord** [God], and spake of **him** [Jesus] to all them that looked for redemption in Jerusalem."

2:40   "And the **child** [Jesus] grew, and waxed strong in spirit, filled with wisdom: and the grace of **God** was upon him."

2:49   "And **he** [Jesus] said unto them, How is it that ye sought me? wist ye not that I must be about my **Father's** business?"

2:52   "And **Jesus** increased in wisdom and stature, and in favour with **God** and man."

3:21-22   "...**Jesus** also being baptized, and praying, the heaven was opened...and a voice came from heaven, which said, Thou art **my** [God's] beloved Son; in thee I am well pleased."

4:4   "And **Jesus** answered him, saying, It is written, That man shall not live by bread alone, but by every word of **God**."

4:8   "And **Jesus** answered and said unto him, Get thee behind me, Satan: for it is written, Thou shalt worship the Lord thy **God**, and him only shalt thou serve."

4:12   "And **Jesus** answering said unto him, It is said, Thou shalt not tempt [put to the test] the Lord thy **God**."

4:18   "The Spirit of the **Lord** [God] is upon **me** [Jesus] because he hath anointed me to preach the gospel to the poor... ."

4:41   "...Thou art **Christ** the Son of **God**...for they knew that he was Christ."

4:43   "And **he** [Jesus] said unto them, I must preach the kingdom of **God** to other cities also: for therefore am I sent."

5:1   "And it came to pass, that, as the people pressed upon **him** [Jesus] to hear the word of **God**, he stood by the lake of Gennesaret... ."

5:17   "And it came to pass on a certain day, as **he** [Jesus] was teaching...the power of the **Lord** [God] was present to heal them."

5:24-25   "...**I** [Jesus] say unto thee, Arise, and take up thy couch, and go into thine house. And immediately he rose up before them...and departed to his own house, glorifying **God**."

6:3-4   "And **Jesus** answering them said, Have ye not read so much as this, what David did...How he went into the house of **God**, and did take and eat the shewbread... ."

6:12 "And it came to pass in those days, that **he** [Jesus] went out into a mountain to pray, and continued all night in prayer to **God**."

6:20 "And **he** [Jesus] lifted up his eyes on his disciples, and said, Blessed be ye poor: for yours is the kingdom of **God**."

6:27,35 "But **I** [Jesus] say unto you which hear, Love your enemies...and ye shall be the children of the **Highest** [God]: for he is kind unto the unthankful and to the evil."

7:15-16 "And **he** [Jesus] delivered him to his mother. And there came a fear on all: and they glorified **God**, saying, That a great prophet is risen up among us... ."

7:27 "This is he [John] of whom it is written, Behold, **I** [God] send my messenger before **thy** [Jesus'] face, which shall prepare thy way before thee."

7:28 "For **I** [Jesus] say unto you...he that is least in the kingdom of **God** is greater than he."

8:1 "And it came to pass afterward, that **he** [Jesus] went throughout every city and village, preaching and shewing the glad tidings of the kingdom of **God**... ."

8:10   "And **he** [Jesus] said, Unto you it is given to know the mysteries of the kingdom of **God**: but to others in parables... ."

8:21   "And **he** [Jesus] answered and said unto them, My mother and my brethren are these which hear the word of **God**, and do it."

8:38-39   "...but **Jesus** sent him away, saying, Return to thine own house, and shew how great things **God** hath done unto thee."

9:2   "And **he** [Jesus] sent them to preach the kingdom of **God**, and to heal the sick."

9:11   "And the people, when they knew it, followed **him** [Jesus], and he received them, and spake unto them of the kingdom of **God**, and healed them... ."

9:20   "He [Jesus] said unto them, But whom say ye that I am? Peter answering said, The **Christ** [Messiah] of **God**."

9:26   "For whosoever shall be ashamed of me and of my words, of him shall the **Son of man** be ashamed, when he shall come in his own glory, and in his **Father's**, and of the holy angels."

9:27   "But **I** [Jesus] tell you of a truth, there be some standing here, which shall not taste of death, till they see the kingdom of **God**."

9:35-36   "And there came a voice out of the cloud, saying, This is **my** [God's] beloved Son: hear him. And when the voice was past, **Jesus** was found alone."

9:42-43   "And **Jesus** rebuked the unclean spirit, and healed the child, and delivered him again to his father. And they were all amazed at the mighty power of **God**."

9:47-48   "And **Jesus**...took a child, and set him by him, And said unto them...whosoever shall receive me receiveth **him** [God] that sent me... ."

9:60   "**Jesus** said unto him, Let the dead bury their dead: but go thou and preach the kingdom of **God**."

9:62   "And **Jesus** said unto him, No man, having put his hand to the plough, and looking back, is fit for the kingdom of **God**."

10:2   "Therefore said **he** [Jesus] unto them, The harvest truly is great, but the labourers are few: pray ye therefore the **Lord** [God] of the harvest, that he would send forth labourers into his harvest."

10:16   "...he that despiseth **me** [Jesus] despiseth **him** [God] that sent me."

10:21   "In that hour **Jesus** rejoiced in spirit, and said, I thank thee, O **Father**, Lord of heaven and earth, that thou hast hid these things from the wise and prudent, and hast revealed them unto babes: even so, Father; for so it seemed good in thy sight."

10:22   "All things are delivered to **me** [Jesus] of my **Father**... ."

10:27   "And **he** [Jesus] answering said, Thou shalt love the Lord thy **God** with all thy heart, and with all thy soul, and with all thy strength, and with all thy mind... ."

11:2   "And **he** [Jesus] said unto them, When ye pray, say, Our **Father** which art in heaven, Hallowed be thy name. Thy kingdom come. Thy will be done, as in heaven, so in earth."

11:9,13   "And **I** [Jesus] say unto you... If ye then, being evil, know how to give good gifts unto your children: how much more shall your heavenly **Father** give the Holy Spirit to them that ask him?"

11:20   "But if **I** [Jesus] with the finger of **God** cast out devils, no doubt the kingdom of God is come upon you."

11:28   "But **he** [Jesus] said, Yea rather, blessed are they that hear the word of **God**, and keep it."

11:39-40   "And the **Lord** [Jesus] said unto him, Now do ye Pharisees make clean the outside of the cup and the platter...Ye fools, did not **he** [God] that made that which is without make that which is within also?"

11:46,49   "And **he** [Jesus] said, Woe unto you...Therefore also said the wisdom of **God**, I will send them prophets and apostles, and some of them they shall slay and persecute... ."

12:5   "But **I** [Jesus] will forewarn you whom ye shall fear: Fear **him** [God], which after he hath killed hath power to cast into hell; yea, I say unto you, Fear **him**."

12:8   "Also I say unto you, Whosoever shall confess me before men, him shall the **Son of man** also confess before the angels of **God**... ."

12:9   "But he that denieth **me** [Jesus] before men shall be denied before the angels of **God**."

12:10   "And whosoever shall speak a word against the **Son of man**, it shall be forgiven him: but unto him that blasphemeth against the **Holy Ghost** [Spirit of God] it shall not be forgiven."

12:22,24   "And **he** [Jesus] said unto his disciples...Consider the ravens: for they neither sow nor reap...and **God** feedeth them... ."

12:27-28   "Consider the lilies how they grow: they toil not, they spin not; and yet **I** [Jesus] say unto you, that Solomon in all his glory was not arrayed like one of these. If then **God** so clothe the grass...how much more will he clothe you, O ye of little faith?"

13:12-13   "And when **Jesus** saw her, he called her to him, and said unto her, Woman, thou art loosed from thine infirmity. And he laid his hands on her: and immediately she was made straight, and glorified **God**."

13:18   "Then said **he** [Jesus], Unto what is the kingdom of **God** like?"

13:20   "And again [Jesus] **he** said, Whereunto shall I liken the kingdom of **God**?"

13:35   "... Ye shall not see **me** [Jesus], until the time come when ye shall say, Blessed is he that cometh in the name of The **Lord** [God]."

16:15   "And **he** [Jesus] said unto them...God knoweth your hearts: for that which is highly esteemed among men is abomination in the sight of **God**."

17:14-15   "And when **he** [Jesus] saw them, he said unto them, Go shew yourselves unto the priests. And it came to pass, that, as they went, they were cleansed. And one of them...with a loud voice glorified **God**... ."

17:20   "And when he was demanded of the Pharisees, when the kingdom of God should come, **he** [Jesus] answered them and said, The kingdom of **God** cometh not with observation."

18:1-2   "And **he** [Jesus] spake a parable unto them to this end, that men ought always to pray, and not to faint; Saying, There was in a city a judge, which feared not **God**... ."

18:6-7   "And the **Lord** [Jesus] said, Hear what the unjust judge saith. And shall not **God** avenge his own elect, which cry day and night unto him... ."

18:8   "I tell you that **he** [God] will avenge them speedily. Nevertheless when the **Son of man** cometh, shall he find faith on the earth?"

18:9-11   "And **he** [Jesus] spake this parable unto certain which trusted in themselves that they were righteous, and despised others...The Pharisee stood and prayed thus with himself, **God**, I thank thee, that I am not as other men are... ."

18:13-14   "And the publican, standing afar off...saying, **God** be merciful to me a sinner. **I** [Jesus] tell you, this man went down to his house justified rather than the other... ."

18:16   "But **Jesus** called them unto him, and said, Suffer little children to come unto me, and forbid them not: for of such is the kingdom of **God**."

18:17   "Verily **I** [Jesus] say unto you, Whosoever shall not receive the kingdom of **God** as a little child shall in no wise enter therein."

18:19   "And **Jesus** said unto him, Why callest thou me good? none is good, save one, that is, **God**."

18:24   "And when **Jesus** saw that he was very sorrowful, he said, How hardly shall they that have riches enter into the kingdom of **God**!"

18:27   "And **he** [Jesus] said, The things which are impossible with men are possible with **God**."

18:29   "And **he** [Jesus] said unto them, Verily I say unto you, There is no man that hath left house, or parents, or brethren, or wife, or children, for the kingdom of **God's** sake, Who shall not receive manifold more... ."

18:42-43   "And **Jesus** said unto him, Receive thy sight... And immediately he received his sight, and followed him, glorifying **God**: and all the people, when they saw it, gave praise unto God."

19:11   "And as they heard these things, **he** [Jesus] added and spake a parable... because they thought that the kingdom of **God** should immediately appear."

19:37   "And when **he** [Jesus] was come nigh, even now at the descent of the mount of Olives, the whole multitude of the disciples began to rejoice and praise **God** with a loud voice for all the mighty works that they had seen... ."

19:38   "... Blessed be the **King** [Jesus] that cometh in the name of the **Lord** [God], peace in heaven, and glory in the highest."

19:45-46   "And **he** [Jesus] went into the temple, and began to cast out them that sold therein, and them that bought; Saying unto them, It is written, **My** [God's] house is the house of prayer: but ye have made it a den of thieves."

20:21   "...**Master**, we know that thou sayest and teachest rightly, neither acceptest thou the person of any, but teachest the way of **God** truly... ."

20:25   "And **he** [Jesus] said unto them, Render therefore unto Caesar the things which be Caesar's, and unto **God** the things which be God's."

20:34-36   "And **Jesus** answering said unto them, The children of this world marry...But they which shall be accounted worthy to obtain that world...neither marry, nor are given in marriage...for they are equal unto the angels; and are the children of **God**, being the children of the resurrection."

20:38-39   "For he is not a **God** of the dead, but of the living: for all live unto him. Then certain of the scribes answering said, **Master**, thou hast well said."

20:41-42   "And he said unto them, How say they that Christ is David's son? And David himself saith in the book of Psalms, The **Lord** [God] said unto my **Lord** [Jesus], Sit thou on my right hand, Till I make thine enemies thy footstool."

21:3-4   "And he said, Of a truth **I** [Jesus] say unto you...all these have of their abundance cast in unto the offerings of **God**: but she of her penury hath cast in all the living that she had."

22:16   "For I say unto you, **I** [Jesus] will not any more eat thereof, until it be fulfilled in the kingdom of **God**."

22:18   "For I say unto you, I [Jesus] will not drink of the fruit of the vine, until the kingdom of God shall come."

22:29   "And I appoint unto you a kingdom, as my Father hath appointed unto me [Jesus]... ."

22:41-42 "And he [Jesus] was withdrawn from them about a stone's cast, and kneeled down, and prayed, Saying, Father, if thou be willing, remove this cup from me: nevertheless not my will, but thine, be done."

22:69   "Hereafter shall the Son of man sit on the right hand of the power of God."

23:34   "Then said Jesus, [heavenly] Father, forgive them; for they know not what they do."

23:46   "And when Jesus had cried with a loud voice, he said, Father, into thy hands I commend my spirit: and having said thus, he gave up the ghost."

24:19   "...And they said unto him, Concerning Jesus of Nazareth, which was a prophet mighty in deed and word before God and all the people... ."

24:49   "And, behold, I [Jesus] send the promise of my Father upon you: but tarry ye in the city of Jerusalem, until ye be endued with power from on high."

Paul's Prayer

*"That **the God of our Lord Jesus Christ, the Father** of glory, may give unto you the spirit of wisdom and revelation in the knowledge of **him**: The eyes of your understanding being enlightened; that ye may know what is the hope of **his** calling, and what the riches of the glory of **his** inheritance in the saints, And what is the exceeding greatness of **his** power to us-ward who believe, according to the working of **his** mighty power, Which **he** wrought in Christ, when **he** raised him from the dead, and set him **at his own right hand in the heavenly places"** (Ephesians 1:17-20).*

Chapter 4

John

T he gospel of John contains one hundred-sixty-seven passages that make a clear distinction between God and Jesus. They are:

1:14   "...and we beheld **his** [Jesus] glory, the glory as of the only begotten of the **Father**, full of grace and truth."

1:18   "No man hath seen **God** at any time; the only begotten **Son**...hath declared him."

1:29   "The next day John seeth **Jesus** coming unto him, and saith, Behold the Lamb of **God**, which taketh away the sin of the world."

1:36   "And looking upon **Jesus** as he walked, he saith, Behold the Lamb of **God**!"

1:49   "Nathanael answered and saith unto **him** [Jesus], Rabbi, thou art the Son of **God**; thou art the King of Israel."

1:51   "...Hereafter ye shall see heaven open, and the angels of **God** ascending and descending upon the **Son of man**."

2:16   "And [Jesus] said unto them that sold doves...make not **my** [Jesus'] **Father's** house an house of merchandise."

2:17   "And **his** [Jesus'] disciples remembered that it was written, The zeal of **thine** [God's] house hath eaten me up."

3:2   "The same came to **Jesus** by night, and said unto him, Rabbi, we know that thou art a teacher come from **God**: for no man can do these miracles that thou doest, except God be with him."

3:3   "**Jesus** answered and said unto him...Except a man be born again, he cannot see the kingdom of **God**."

3:5   "**Jesus** answered... Except a man be born of water and of the Spirit, he cannot enter into the kingdom of **God**."

3:16   "For **God** so loved the world, that he gave his only begotten **Son**, that whosoever believeth in him should not perish, but have everlasting life."

3:17   "For **God** sent not his **Son** into the world to condemn the world... ."

3:34   "For **he** [Jesus] whom **God** hath sent speaketh the words of God... ."

3:35   "The **Father** loveth the **Son**, and hath given all things into his hand."

3:36   "He that believeth on the **Son** hath everlasting life: and he that believeth not the Son shall not see life; but the wrath of **God** abideth on him."

4:10   "**Jesus** answered and said unto her, If thou knewest the gift of **God**... ."

4:21,23   "**Jesus** saith unto her, Woman, believe me...the hour cometh, and now is, when the true worshippers shall worship the **Father** in spirit and in truth: for the Father seeketh such to worship him."

4:25-26   "**God** is a Spirit...The woman saith unto him, I know that Messias cometh, which is called Christ...**Jesus** saith unto her, I that speak unto thee am he."

4:34   "**Jesus** saith unto them, My meat is to do the will of **him** [God] that sent me, and to finish his work."

5:17   "But **Jesus** answered them, My **Father** worketh hitherto, and I work."

5:19   "Then answered **Jesus** and said unto them, Verily, verily, I say unto you, The Son can do nothing of himself, but what he seeth the **Father** do... ."

5:20   "For the **Father** loveth the **Son**, and sheweth him all things that himself doeth... ."

5:21   "For as the **Father** raiseth up the dead, and quickeneth them; even so the **Son** quickeneth whom he will."

5:22   "For the **Father** judgeth no man, but hath committed all judgment unto the **Son**... ."

5:23   "...He that honoureth not the **Son** honoureth not the **Father** which hath sent him."

5:24   "...He that heareth **my** [Jesus'] word, and believeth on **him** [God] that sent me, hath everlasting life... ."

5:26-27 "... as the **Father** hath life in himself; so hath he given to the **Son** to have life in himself...he is the Son of man."

5:30   "I can of mine own self do nothing... I seek not **mine** [Jesus'] own will, but the will of the **Father** which hath sent me."

5:31-32 "If I bear witness of **myself** [Jesus], my witness is not true. There is another that beareth witness of me; and I know that the witness which **he** [God the Father] witnesseth of me is true."

5:36   "...the works which the **Father** hath given **me** [Jesus] to finish, the same works that I do, bear witness of me, that the Father hath sent me."

5:37   "And the **Father** himself, which hath sent **me** [Jesus], hath borne witness of me. Ye have neither heard his voice at any time, nor seen his shape."

5:38   "And ye have not **his** [God's] word abiding in you: for whom he hath sent, **him** [Jesus] ye believe not."

5:41-42 "**I** [Jesus] receive not honour from men. But I know you, that ye have not the love of **God** in you."

5:43   "**I** [Jesus] am come in my **Father's** name [authority], and ye receive me not... ."

5:45   "Do not think that **I** [Jesus] will accuse you to the **Father**: there is one that accuseth you, even Moses, in whom ye trust."

6:27   "Labour...for that meat which endureth unto everlasting life, which the **Son of man** shall give unto you: for him hath **God** the Father sealed."

6:29   "**Jesus** answered and said unto them, This is the work of **God**, that ye believe on him whom he hath sent."

6:32   "Then **Jesus** said unto them...my **Father** giveth you the true bread from heaven."

6:37   "All that the **Father** giveth **me** [Jesus] shall come to me; and him that cometh to me I will in no wise cast out."

6:39   "And this is the **Father's** will which hath sent **me** [Jesus], that of all which he hath given me I should lose nothing... ."

6:40   "And this is the will of **him** [God] that sent **me** [Jesus],that every one which seeth the Son, and believeth on him, may have everlasting life... ."

6:44   "No man can come to **me** [Jesus], except the **Father** which hath sent me draw him... ."

6:45   "...And they shall be all taught of **God**. Every man therefore that hath heard, and hath learned of the **Father**, cometh unto **me** [Jesus]."

6:46   "Not that any man hath seen the Father, save **he** [Jesus] which is of **God**, he hath seen the Father."

6:57   "As the living **Father** hath sent **me** [Jesus], and I live by the Father: so he that eateth me, even he shall live by me."

6:65   "...Therefore said **I** [Jesus] unto you, that no man can come unto me, except it were given unto him of my **Father**."

6:69   "And we believe and are sure that thou art that **Christ**, the Son of the living **God**."

7:16   "**Jesus** answered them, and said, My doctrine is not mine, but **his** that sent me."

7:17   "If any man will do **his** [God's] will, he shall know of the doctrine, whether it be of God, or whether I speak of **myself** [Jesus]."

7:18   "He that speaketh of himself seeketh his own glory: but **he** [Jesus] that seeketh **his** [God's] glory that sent him, the same is true, and no unrighteousness is in him [Jesus]."

7:28   "Then cried **Jesus** in the temple as he taught, saying...I am not come of myself, but **he** [God] that sent me is true, whom ye know not."

7:29   "But **I** know **him** [God], for I am from him, and he hath sent me."

7:33   "Then said **Jesus** unto them...I go unto **him** [God] that sent me."

8:16   "...I am not alone, but I [Jesus] and the Father that sent me."

8:18   "I am one that bear witness of myself [Jesus], and the Father that sent me beareth witness of me."

8:19   "Jesus answered, Ye neither know me, nor my Father... ."

8:26-27 "I [Jesus] have many things to say and to judge of you: but he that sent me is true...They understood not that he spake to them of the Father."

8:28   "Then said Jesus unto them... I do nothing of myself; but as my Father hath taught me, I speak these things."

8:29   "And he that sent me [Jesus] is with me: the Father hath not left me alone; for I do always those things that please him."

8:38   "I [Jesus] speak that which I have seen with my Father... ."

8:40   "But now ye seek to kill me [Jesus], a man that hath told you the truth, which I have heard of God... ."

8:42   "Jesus said unto them...I proceeded forth and came from God; neither came I of myself, but he sent me."

8:49   "**Jesus** answered...I honour my **Father**, and ye do dishonour me."

8:50   "And **I** [Jesus] seek not mine own glory: there is **one** [God] that seeketh and judgeth."

8:54   "**Jesus** answered, If I honour myself, my honour is nothing: it is my **Father** that honoureth me... ."

8:55   "Yet ye have not known **him** [God], but **I** [Jesus] know him...I know him and keep his saying."

9:3   "**Jesus** answered, Neither hath this man sinned, nor his parents: but that the works of **God** should be made manifest in him."

9:4   "**I** [Jesus] must work the works of **him** [God] that sent me, while it is day... ."

9:35   "**Jesus** heard that they had cast him out; and when he had found him, he said unto him, Dost thou believe on the Son of **God**?"

10:15   "As the **Father** knoweth **me** [Jesus], even so know I the Father... ."

10:17   "Therefore doth my **Father** love **me** [Jesus], because I lay down my life... ."

10:18   "I [Jesus] have power to lay it down (life), and I have power to take it again. This commandment have I received of my **Father**."

10:25   "**Jesus** answered them, I told you, and ye believed not: the works that I do in my **Father's** name, they bear witness of me."

\

10:29   "My **Father**, which gave them **me** [Jesus], is greater than all; and no man is able to pluck them out of my Father's hand."

10:30   "**I** and my **Father** are one." Note: This is in no way a claim by Jesus that he and the Father are one person! He explains his statement himself in John chapter seventeen, verses 11, and 21-23.

10:32   "**Jesus** answered them, Many good works have I shewed you from my **Father**... ."

10:35-36   "If he called them gods, unto whom the word of **God** came, and the scripture cannot be broken; Say ye of **him** [Jesus], whom the **Father** hath sanctified, and sent into the world, Thou blasphemest; because I said, I am the Son of God?"

10:37   "If **I** [Jesus] do not the works of my **Father**, believe me not."

11:4   "When **Jesus** heard that, he said, This sickness is not unto death, but for the glory of **God**... ."

11:22   "But I [Martha] know, that even now, whatsoever **thou** [Jesus] wilt ask of **God**, God will give it thee."

11:27   "She [Martha] saith unto him, Yea, Lord: I believe that thou art the **Christ**, the Son of **God**, which should come into the world."

11:40   "**Jesus** saith unto her, Said I not unto thee, that, if thou wouldest believe, thou shouldest see the glory of **God**?"

11:41   "...And **Jesus** lifted up his eyes, and said, **Father**, I thank thee that thou hast heard me."

11:42   "And I knew that **thou** [God] hearest **me** [Jesus] always: but because of the people which stand by I said it... ."

11:51-52 "...being high priest that year, he prophesied that **Jesus** should die for that nation...but that also he should gather together in one the children of **God** that were scattered abroad."

12:13   "...Blessed is the **King of Israel** [Jesus] that cometh in the name of the **Lord** [God]."

12:27   "...**Father**, save **me** [Jesus] from this hour: but for this cause came I unto this hour."

12:30   "**Jesus** answered and said, **This voice** [of God] came not because of me, but for your sakes."

12:44   "**Jesus** cried and said, He that believeth on me, believeth not on me, but on **him** [God] that sent me."

12:49   "For I have not spoken of **myself** [Jesus]; but the **Father** which sent me, he gave me a commandment, what I should say, and what I should speak."

12:50   "...whatsoever I speak therefore, even as the **Father** said unto **me** [Jesus] so I speak."

13:1   "...**Jesus** knew that his hour was come that he should depart out of this world unto the **Father**... ."

13:3-4   "**Jesus** knowing that the Father had given all things into his hands, and that he was come from **God**, and went to God; He riseth from supper... ."

13:20   "...He that receiveth whomsoever I send receiveth me; and he that receiveth **me** [Jesus] receiveth **him** [God] that sent me."

13:31   "...**Jesus** said, Now is the Son of man glorified, and **God** is glorified in him."

13:32   "If God be glorified in him [Jesus], God shall also glorify him in himself, and shall straightway glorify him".

14:1   "Let not your heart be troubled: ye believe in God, believe also in me [Jesus]."

14:2   "In my Father's house are many mansions: if it were not so, I [Jesus] would have told you."

14:6   "Jesus saith unto him, I am the way, the truth, and the life: no man cometh unto the Father, but by me."

14:7   "If ye had known me [Jesus], ye should have known my Father also... ."

14:10   "... the words that I speak unto you I speak not of myself [Jesus]: but the Father that dwelleth in me, he doeth the works."

14:12   "...He that believeth on me [Jesus], the works that I do shall he do also; and greater works than these shall he do; because I go unto my Father."

14:13   "And whatsoever ye shall ask in my name, that will I do, that the Father may be glorified in the Son."

14:16   "And I [Jesus] will pray the Father, and he shall give you another Comforter... ."

14:20   "At that day ye shall know that **I** [Jesus] am in my **Father**, and ye in me, and I in you."

14:21   "He that hath my commandments, and keepeth them, he it is that loveth me: and he that loveth **me** [Jesus] shall be loved of my **Father**... ."

14:23   "**Jesus** answered and said unto him, If a man love me, he will keep my words: and my **Father** will love him... ."

14:24   "...the word which ye hear is not **mine**, but the **Father's** which sent me."

14:26   "But the Comforter, which is the Holy Ghost, whom the **Father** will send in **my** [Jesus'] name, he shall teach you all things... ."

14:28   "If ye loved me ye would rejoice, because I said, **I** [Jesus] go unto the **Father**: for my Father is greater than I."

14:31   "But that the world may know that **I** [Jesus] love the **Father**; and as the Father gave me commandment, even so I do."

15:1   "**I** [Jesus] am the true vine, and my **Father** is the husbandman."

15:2   "Every branch in **me** [Jesus] that beareth not fruit **he** [God] taketh away... ."

15:8   "Herein is my **Father** glorified, that ye bear much fruit; so shall ye be **my** [Jesus'] disciples."

15:9   "As the **Father** hath loved **me** [Jesus], so have I loved you: continue ye in my love."

15:10   "If ye keep **my** [Jesus] commandments ye shall abide in my love; even as I have kept my **Father's** commandments, and abide in his love."

15:15   "...for all things that **I** [Jesus] have heard of my **Father** I have made known unto you."

15:16   "...your fruit should remain: that whatsoever ye shall ask of the **Father** in **my** [Jesus] name, he may give it you."

15:23   "He that hateth **me** [Jesus] hateth my **Father** also."

15:24   "...now have they both seen and hated both **me** [Jesus] and my **Father**."

15:26   "But when the Comforter is come, whom **I** [Jesus] will send unto you from the **Father**, even the Spirit of truth, which proceedeth from the Father, he shall testify of me... ."

16:1-2   "These things have I [Jesus] spoken unto you...yea, the time cometh, that whosoever killeth you will think that he doeth God service."

16:3   "And these things will they do unto you, because they have not known the Father, nor me [Jesus]."

16:5   "But now I go my way to him [God] that sent me [Jesus]... ."

16:10   "Of righteousness, because I [Jesus] go to my Father, and ye see me no more... ."

16:15   "All things that the Father hath are mine [Jesus']... ."

16:16   "A little while, and ye shall not see me [Jesus]...because I go to the Father."

16:17   "...What is this that he [Jesus] saith unto us...Because I go to the Father?"

16:23   "And in that day ye shall ask me [Jesus] nothing. Verily, verily, I say unto you, Whatsoever ye shall ask the Father in my name, he will give it you."

16:25   "...but the time cometh, when I [Jesus] shall no more speak unto you in proverbs, but I shall shew you plainly of the Father."

16:26   "At that day ye shall ask in **my** [Jesus] name: and I say not unto you, that I will pray the **Father** for you... ."

16:27   "For the Father himself loveth you, because ye have loved **me** [Jesus], and have believed that I came out from **God**."

16:28   "**I** [Jesus] came forth from the **Father**, and am come into the world: again, I leave the world, and go to the Father."

16:30   "... by this we believe that **thou** [Jesus] camest forth from **God**."

16:32   "...I [Jesus] am not alone, because the **Father** is with me."

17:1   "These words spake **Jesus**, and lifted up his eyes to heaven, and said, **Father**, the hour is come; glorify thy Son... ."

17:2   "As **thou** [God] hast given **him** [Jesus] power over all flesh... ."

17:3   "And this is life eternal, that they might know thee the only true **God**, and **Jesus Christ**, whom thou hast sent."

17:4   "**I** [Jesus] have glorified **thee** [God] on the earth: I have finished the work which thou gavest me to do."

17:5   "And now, O **Father**, glorify thou **me** [Jesus] with thine own self... ."

17:6   "**I** [Jesus] have manifested **thy** [God's] name unto the men which thou gavest me out of the world... ."

17:7   "Now they have known that all things whatsoever thou hast given **me** [Jesus] are of **thee** [God]."

17:8   "For I have given unto them the words which **thou** [God] gavest **me** [Jesus]... ."

17:9   "I pray not for the world, but for them which **thou** [God] hast given **me** [Jesus]... ."

17:10   "And all **mine** [Jesus] are **thine** [God], and thine are mine... ."

17:11   "...Holy **Father**, keep through thine own name those whom thou hast given **me** [Jesus], that they may be one, as we are."

17:12   "While I was with them in the world, **I** [Jesus] kept them in **thy** [God's] name... ."

17:13   "And now come **I** [Jesus] to **thee** [God]... ."

17:14   "**I** [Jesus] have given them **thy** [God's] word... ."

17:15   "**I** [Jesus] pray not that **thou** [God] shouldest take them out of the world... ."

17:18   "As **thou** [God] hast sent **me** [Jesus] into the world, even so have I also sent them into the world."

17:21   "That they all may be one; as thou, **Father**, art in **me** [Jesus], and I in thee, that they also may be one in us... ."

17:22   "And the glory which **thou** [God] gavest **me** [Jesus] I have given them; that they may be one, even as we are one... ."

17:23   "I in them, and thou in me, that they may be made perfect in one; and that the world may know that **thou** [God] hast sent **me** [Jesus], and hast loved them, as thou hast loved me."

17:24   "**Father**, I will that they also, whom thou hast given **me** [Jesus], be with me where I am... ."

17:25   "O righteous **Father**, the world hath not known thee: but **I** [Jesus] have known thee... ."

17:26   "And **I** [Jesus] have declared unto them **thy** [God's] name, and will declare it... ."

18:11   "Then said **Jesus** unto Peter...the cup which my **Father** hath given me, shall I not drink it?"

19:11   "**Jesus** answered, Thou couldest have no power at all against me, except it were given thee from **above** [God]... ."

20:17   "**Jesus** saith unto her, Touch me not; for I am not yet ascended to my **Father**: but go to my brethren, and say unto them, I ascend unto my Father, and your Father; and to my **God**, and your **God**."

20:21   "Then said **Jesus** to them again, Peace be unto you: as my **Father** hath sent me, even so send I you."

20:31   "But these [John's writings] are written, that ye might believe that **Jesus** is the Christ, the Son of **God**; and that believing ye might have life through his name."

21:19   "This spake **he** [Jesus] signifying by what death he [Peter] should glorify **God**."

Chapter 5

Acts

*T*he book of Acts contains fifty-six passages that make a clear distinction between God and Jesus. They are:

1:3   "To whom also **he** [Jesus] shewed himself alive after his passion...speaking of the things pertaining to the kingdom of **God**... ."

1:4   "... but wait for the promise of the **Father**, which, saith **he** [Jesus] ye have heard of me."

1:7   "And **he** [Jesus] said unto them, It is not for you to know the times or the seasons, which the **Father** hath put in his own power."

2:22   "...**Jesus** of Nazareth, a man approved of **God** among you by miracles and wonders and signs, which God did by him... ."

2:23   "**Him** [Jesus] being delivered by the determinate counsel and foreknowledge of **God**, ye have...crucified... ."

2:24   "Whom **God** hath raised up, having loosed the pains of death: because it was not possible that **he** [Jesus] should be holden of it."

2:26-27   "Therefore did **my** [Jesus'] heart rejoice...Because **thou** [God] wilt not leave my soul in hell, neither wilt thou suffer thine Holy One to see corruption."

2:28   "**Thou** [God] hast made known to **me** [Jesus] the ways of life; thou shalt make me full of joy with thy countenance."

2:30   "Therefore being a prophet [David], and knowing that God had sworn with an oath to him, that...**he** [God] would raise up **Christ** to sit on his [David's] throne... ."

2:32   "This **Jesus** hath **God** raised up, whereof we all are witnesses ."

2:33   "Therefore being by the right hand of **God** exalted, and having received of the Father the promise of the Holy Ghost, **he** [Jesus] hath shed forth this, which ye now see and hear."

2:34-35   "...but he saith himself, The **Lord** [God] said unto my **Lord** [Jesus], Sit thou on my right hand, Until I make thy foes thy footstool."

2:36   "...**God** hath made that same **Jesus**, whom ye have crucified, both Lord and Christ."

2:38-39   "Then Peter said unto them, Repent, and be baptized every one of you in the name of **Jesus** Christ...even as many as the Lord our **God** shall call."

3:6,9   "Then Peter said... In the name of **Jesus** Christ of Nazareth rise up and walk. And all the people saw him walking and praising **God**."

3:13   "The **God** of Abraham, and of Isaac, and of Jacob, the God of our fathers, hath glorified his Son **Jesus**."

3:15   "And killed the **Prince of life** [Jesus], whom **God** hath raised from the dead... ."

3:18   "But those things, which **God** before had shewed by the mouth of all his prophets, that **Christ** should suffer, he hath so fulfilled."

3:20   "And **he** [God] shall send **Jesus** Christ, which before was preached unto you... ."

3:22   "For Moses truly said unto the fathers, **A prophet** [Jesus] shall the Lord your **God** raise up unto you of your brethren, like unto me... ."

3:23   "**Him** [Jesus] being delivered by the determinate counsel and foreknowledge of **God**, ye have...crucified... ."

69

3:24   "Whom **God** hath raised up, having loosed the pains of
            death: because it was not possible that **he** [Jesus]
            should be holden of it."

3:26   "Unto you first **God**, having raised up his Son **Jesus**,
            sent him to bless you... ."

4:10   "Be it known unto you all...that by the name of **Jesus**
            Christ of Nazareth, whom ye crucified, whom **God**
            raised from the dead... ."

4:26   "The kings of the earth stood up, and the rulers were
            gathered together against the **Lord** [God] and against
            his **Christ**."

4:27   "For of a truth against thy holy child **Jesus**, whom
            thou [God] hast anointed...the people of Israel, were
            gathered together... ."

4:29-30   "And now, **Lord** [God]...By stretching forth thine hand
            to heal; and that signs and wonders may be done by the
            name of thy holy child **Jesus**."

5:30   "The **God** of our fathers raised up **Jesus**, whom ye
            slew and hanged on a tree."

5:31   "**Him** [Jesus] hath **God** exalted with his right hand to
            be a Prince and a Saviour... ."

70

7:37   "This is that Moses, which said unto the children of Israel, **A prophet** [Jesus] shall the Lord your **God** raise up unto you of your brethren, like unto me; him [Jesus] shall ye hear."

7:55   "But he [Stephen]...looked up stedfastly into heaven, and saw the glory of **God**, and **Jesus** standing on the right hand of **God**... ."

7:56   "Behold, I see the heavens opened, and the **Son of man** standing on the right hand of **God**."

8:12   "But when they believed Philip preaching the things concerning the kingdom of **God**, and the name of **Jesus** Christ, they were baptized, both men and women."

8:37   "...And he answered and said, I believe that **Jesus** Christ is the Son of **God**."

9:20   "And straightway he [Saul-Paul] preached **Christ** in the synagogues, that he is the Son of **God**."

10:36   "The word which **God** sent unto the children of Israel, preaching peace by **Jesus** Christ... ."

10:38   "How **God** anointed **Jesus** of Nazareth with the Holy Ghost and with power: who went about doing good...for **God** was with **him**."

10:40   "**Him** [Jesus] **God** raised up the third day, and shewed him openly... ."

10:41   "...witnesses chosen before of **God**, even to us, who did eat and drink with **him** [Jesus] after he rose from the dead."

10:42   "And **he** [Jesus] commanded us to preach unto the people, and to testify that it is he which was ordained of **God** to be the Judge of quick and dead."

11:17   "Forasmuch then as **God** gave them the like gift as he did unto us, who believed on the Lord **Jesus** Christ; what was I, that I could withstand God?"

13:23   "Of this man's seed hath **God** according to his promise raised unto Israel a Saviour, **Jesus**... ."

13:30   "But **God** raised **him** [Jesus] from the dead... ."

13:33   "**God** hath fulfilled the same unto us their children, in that he hath raised up **Jesus** again... ."

13:37   "But **he** [Jesus], whom **God** raised again, saw no corruption."

15:10-11 "Now therefore why tempt ye **God**...But we believe that through the grace of the Lord **Jesus** Christ we shall be saved, even as they."

72

16:17-18   "The same followed Paul and us, and cried, saying, These men are the servants of the most high **God**...But Paul, being grieved, turned and said to the spirit, I command thee in the name of **Jesus** Christ to come out of her."

16:31-32   "Believe on the Lord **Jesus** Christ, and thou shalt be saved, and thy house. And they spake unto him the word of the **Lord** [God], and to all that were in his house."

17:30-31   "And the times of this ignorance **God** winked at; but now commandeth all men every where to repent: Because he hath appointed a day, in the which he will judge the world in righteousness by **that man** [Jesus] whom he hath ordained; whereof he hath given assurance unto all men, in that **he** [God] hath raised **him** [Jesus] from the dead."

19:10-11   "...all they which dwelt in Asia heard the word of the Lord **Jesus**, both Jews and Greeks. And **God** wrought special miracles by the hands of Paul... ."

20:21   "Testifying both to the Jews, and also to the Greeks, repentance toward **God**, and faith toward our Lord **Jesus** Christ."

20:24   "...that I might finish my course with joy, and the ministry which I have received of the Lord **Jesus**, to testify the gospel of the grace of **God**."

22:14   "The **God** of our fathers hath chosen thee, that thou shouldest know his will, and see that **Just One** [Jesus]... ."

26:8-9   "Why should it be thought a thing incredible with you, that **God** should raise the dead...**Jesus** of Nazareth."

26:17-18   "Delivering thee from the people...unto whom now **I** [Jesus] send thee [Paul], To open their eyes, and to turn them...unto **God**... ."

26:22-23   "Having therefore obtained help of **God**, I continue unto this day, witnessing both to small and great, saying ...That **Christ** should suffer... ."

28:23   "And when they had appointed him a day...he expounded and testified the kingdom of **God**, persuading them concerning **Jesus**... ."

28:31   "Preaching the kingdom of **God**, and teaching those things which concern the Lord **Jesus** Christ. ."

Chapter 6

Romans

*T*he book of Romans contains forty-seven passages that make a clear distinction between God and Jesus. They are:

1:1   "Paul, a servant of **Jesus** Christ... separated unto the gospel of **God**... ."

1:2-3   "Which **he** [God] had promised afore by his prophets in the holy scriptures, Concerning his Son **Jesus** Christ... ."

1:7   "Grace to you and peace from **God** our Father, and the Lord **Jesus** Christ."

1:8   "First, I thank my **God** through **Jesus** Christ for you all... ."

1:9 "   "For **God** is my witness, whom I serve with my spirit in the gospel of his **Son**... ."

1:16   "For I am not ashamed of the gospel of **Christ**: for it is the power of **God** unto salvation to every one that believeth... ."

2:16   "In the day when **God** shall judge the secrets of men by **Jesus** Christ... ."

3:22 "Even the righteousness of God which is by faith of Jesus Christ unto all... ."

3:25 "[Jesus] Whom God hath set forth to be a propitiation through faith in his [Jesus'] blood... ."

3:26 "To declare, I say, at this time his [God's] righteousness: that he [God] might be just, and the justifier of him which believeth in Jesus."

4:24 "But for us also...if we believe on him [God] that raised up Jesus our Lord from the dead... ."

5:1 "... we have peace with God through our Lord Jesus Christ... ."

5:2 "[Jesus] By whom also we have access by faith into this grace wherein we stand, and rejoice in hope of the glory of God."

5:8 "But God commendeth his love toward us, in that, while we were yet sinners, Christ died for us."

5:10 "For...we were reconciled to God by the death of his Son... ."

5:11 "And not only so, but we also joy in God through our Lord Jesus Christ... ."

5:15   "For if through the offence of one many be dead, much more the grace of **God**, and the gift by grace, which is by one man, **Jesus** Christ, hath abounded unto many."

6:4   "...like as **Christ** was raised up from the dead by the glory of the **Father**, even so we also should walk in newness of life."

6:10   "For in that **he** [Jesus] died, he died unto sin once: but in that he liveth, he [Jesus] liveth unto **God**."

6:11   "Likewise reckon ye also yourselves to be dead indeed unto sin, but alive unto **God** through **Jesus** Christ our Lord."

6:23   "For the wages of sin is death; but the gift of **God** is eternal life through **Jesus** Christ our Lord."

7:4   "Wherefore, my brethren, ye also are become dead to the law by the body of **Christ**...that we should bring forth fruit unto **God**."

7:25   "I thank **God** through **Jesus** Christ our Lord."

8:3   "...**God** sending his own **Son** in the likeness of sinful flesh... ."

8:9   "But ye are not in the flesh, but in the Spirit, if so be that the Spirit of **God** dwell in you. Now if any man have not the Spirit of **Christ**, he is none of his."

8:11   "But if the Spirit of **him** [God] that raised up Jesus from the dead dwell in you, he that raised up **Christ** from the dead shall also quicken your mortal bodies... ."

8:17   "And if children, then heirs; heirs of **God**, and joint-heirs with **Christ**... ."

8:29   "For whom **he** [God] did foreknow, he also did predestinate to be conformed to the image of his **Son**, that he might be the firstborn among many brethren."

8:32   "**He** [God] that spared not his own **Son**, but delivered him up for us all, how shall he not with him also freely give us all things?"

8:34   "It is **Christ** that died..who is even at the right hand of **God**, who also maketh intercession for us."

8:39   "Nor height, nor depth, nor any other creature, shall be able to separate us from the love of **God**, which is in Christ **Jesus** our Lord."

9:5   "...as concerning the flesh **Christ** came...**God** blessed for ever."

9:33   "As it is written, Behold, I [God] lay in Sion a stumblingstone and rock of offence: and whosoever believeth on **him** [Jesus] shall not be ashamed."

10:3-4   "For they...have not submitted themselves unto the righteousness of **God**. For **Christ** is the end of the law for righteousness to every one that believeth."

10:9   "That if thou shalt confess with thy mouth the Lord **Jesus,** and shalt believe in thine heart that **God** hath raised him from the dead, thou shalt be saved."

14:18   "For he that in these things serveth **Christ** is acceptable to **God**, and approved of men."

15:5   "Now the **God** of patience and consolation grant you to be likeminded one toward another according to Christ **Jesus... .**"

15:6   "That ye may with one mind and one mouth glorify **God**, even the Father of our Lord **Jesus** Christ."

15:7   "Wherefore receive ye one another, as **Christ** also received us to the glory of **God**."

15:8   "Now I say that **Jesus** Christ was a minister of the circumcision for the truth of **God... .**"

15:16   "That I should be the minister of Jesus Christ to the Gentiles, ministering the gospel of God... ."

15:17   "I have therefore whereof I may glory through Jesus Christ in those things which pertain to God."

15:19   "Through mighty signs and wonders, by the power of the Spirit of God...I have fully preached the gospel of Christ."

15:30   "Now I beseech you, brethren, for the Lord Jesus Christ's sake...that ye strive together with me in your prayers to God for me... ."

16:20   "And the God of peace shall bruise Satan under your feet shortly. The grace of our Lord Jesus Christ be with you. Amen."

16:25   "Now to him [God] that is of power to stablish you according to my gospel, and the preaching of Jesus Christ... ."

16:27   "To God only wise, be glory through Jesus Christ for ever. Amen."

Chapter 7

First Corinthians

*P*aul's first letter to the Corinthians contains twenty-five passages that make a clear distinction between God and Jesus. They are:

1:1   "Paul, called to be an apostle of **Jesus** Christ through the will of **God**... ."

1:2   "Unto the church of **God** which is at Corinth, to them that are sanctified in Christ **Jesus**, called to be saints... ."

1:3   "Grace be unto you, and peace, from **God** our Father, and from the Lord **Jesus** Christ."

1:4   "I thank my **God** always on your behalf, for the grace of God which is given you by **Jesus** Christ... ."

1:24   "But unto them which are called...**Christ** the power of **God**, and the wisdom of God."

1:30   "But of him are ye in Christ **Jesus**, who of **God** is made unto us wisdom... ."

2:16   "For who hath known the mind of the **Lord** [Isaiah 40:13-YHWH-God] that he may instruct **him** [God]? But we have the mind of **Christ**."

3:22-23   "Whether Paul, or Apollos, or Cephas...all are yours; And ye are Christ's; and **Christ** is **God's**."

4:1   "Let a man so account of us, as of the ministers of **Christ**, and stewards of the mysteries of **God**."

6:11   "...ye are justified in the name of the Lord **Jesus**, and by the Spirit of our **God**."

6:14   "And **God** hath both raised up the **Lord** [Jesus] and will also raise up us by his own power."

6:15   "Know ye not that your bodies are the members of **Christ**? Shall I then take the members of Christ, and make them the members of an harlot? **God** forbid."

8:6   "But to us there is but one **God**, the Father, of whom are all things, and we in him; and one Lord **Jesus** Christ, by whom are all things, and we by him."

9:21   "...(being not without law to **God**, but under the law to **Christ**,) that I might gain them that are without law."

10:4-5   "...and that Rock was **Christ**. But with many of them **God** was not well pleased... ."

11:3   "But I would have you know, that the head of every man is **Christ**...and the head of Christ is **God**."

12:3   "...no man speaking by the Spirit of **God** calleth **Jesus** accursed... ."

12:27-28   "Now ye are the body of **Christ**, and members in particular. And **God** hath set some in the church, first apostles... ."

15:15   "...we have testified of **God** that he raised up **Christ**... ."

15:24   "Then cometh the end, when **he** [Jesus] shall have delivered up the kingdom to **God**, even the Father... ."

15:25   "For **he** [Jesus] must reign, till **he** [God] hath put all enemies under his feet." See Psalms 110:1.

15:27   "But when he saith all things are put under him, it is manifest that **he** [God] is excepted which did put all things under **him** [Jesus]."

15:28   "And when all things shall be subdued unto **him** [Jesus], then shall the Son also himself be subject unto him that put all things under him, that **God** may be all in all."

15:57   "But thanks be to **God**, which giveth us the victory through our Lord **Jesus** Christ."

Paul Defining God

*"We know that an idol is nothing in the world, and that **there is none other God but one**. For though there be that are called gods, **whether in heaven or in earth**, (as there be gods many, and lords many,) **But to us there is but one God, the Father,** of whom are all things, and we in him; and one Lord Jesus Christ, by whom are all things, and we by him. Howbeit there is not in every man that knowledge."*

(I Corinthians 8:4-7)

Chapter 8

Second Corinthians

*P*aul's second letter to the Corinthians contains twenty-five passages that make a clear distinction between God and Jesus. They are:

1:1   "Paul, an apostle of **Jesus** Christ by the will of **God**... ."

1:2   Grace be to you and peace from **God** our Father, and from the Lord **Jesus** Christ."

1:3   "Blessed be **God**, even the Father of our Lord **Jesus** Christ, the Father of mercies, and the God of all comfort... ."

1:18-19   "But as **God** is true, our word toward you was not yea and nay. For the Son of God, **Jesus** Christ, who was preached among you by us... ."

1:20   "For all the promises of **God** in **him** [Jesus] are yea, and in him Amen, unto the glory of God by us."

1:21   "Now he which stablisheth us with you in **Christ**, and hath anointed us, is **God**... ."

2:14   "Now thanks be unto **God**, which always causeth us to triumph in **Christ**... ."

2:15   "For we are unto God a sweet savour of Christ, in them that are saved, and in them that perish... ."

2:17   "...in the sight of God speak we in Christ."

3:3   "...the epistle of Christ ministered by us, written not with ink, but with the Spirit of the living God... ."

3;4-5   "And such trust have we through Christ...but our sufficiency is of God... ."

4:4   "...the light of the glorious gospel of Christ, who is the image of God... ."

4:6   "For God...hath shined in our hearts, to give the light of the knowledge of the glory of God in the face of Jesus Christ."

4:14   "Knowing that he [God] which raised up the Lord Jesus shall raise up us also by Jesus, and shall present us with you."

5:18   "And all things are of God, who hath reconciled us to himself by Jesus Christ... ."

5:19   "To wit, that God was in Christ, reconciling the world unto himself... ." Note: Christians are to be filled with God as well, see Ephesians 3:19.

86

5:20   "Now then we are ambassadors for **Christ**, as though **God** did beseech you by us: we pray you in Christ's stead, be ye reconciled to God."

5:21   "For **he** [God] hath made **him** [Jesus] to be sin for us, who knew no sin; that we might be made the righteousness of God in him."

9:13   "...they glorify **God** for your professed subjection unto the gospel of **Christ**... ."

10:5   "Casting down imaginations, and every high thing that exalteth itself against the knowledge of **God**, and bringing into captivity every thought to the obedience of **Christ**."

11:31   "The **God** and Father of our Lord **Jesus** Christ...knoweth that I lie not."

12:2   "I knew a man in **Christ** above fourteen years ago, (whether in the body, I cannot tell...**God** knoweth;)... ."

12:19   "Again,...we speak before **God** in **Christ**... ."

13:4   "For though **he** [Jesus] was crucified through weakness, yet he liveth by the power of **God**. For we also...shall live with him by the power of God... ."

13:14   "The grace of the Lord Jesus Christ, and the love of God... be with you all. Amen."

Seeing God The Father

Our Father God is **a person** *(Job 13:8; Heb. 1:3)*, who has **a will** *(Luke 22:42; John 5:30)*, **a personality** *(Zeph. 3:17)*, **a shape** *(Num. 12:8; James 3:9)*, **a face** *(Matt. 18:10; Rev. 22:4)*, **a head** and **hair** *(Daniel 7:9)*, **eyes** *(Deut. 11:12; Prov. 15:3; Ps. 34:15)*, **ears** *(Num. 11:18; Isa. 59:1; James 5:4)*, **a mouth** *(Deut. 8:3; Matt. 4:4)*, **breath** *(Ps. 33:6; Gen. 2:7)*, **a voice** *(Gen. 3:8; Deut. 4:12; Heb. 12:25)*, **hands** *(Gen. 49:24; Ex. 15:17; Isa. 5:12)*, **back parts** *(Ex. 33:23)*, **and feet** *(Ex. 24:10; II Sam. 22:10; Isa. 60:13; Nah. 1:3)*. **He loves, laughs, sings, walks, stands, sits, feels** and **thinks. He is not in any way human**, but he has **a heavenly body** (as do angels - *Ps. 104:4; I Cor. 15:40, 44; Heb. 12:9; I Kings 22:19)*, and we are made in His image! Note: Do not be confused by the Bible verses that make reference to the Almighty's wings. This is speaking figuratively as the nations of Assyria and Moab are also said to have wings *(Isa. 8:8; Jer. 48:9;* and the Messiah, Jesus Christ is promised to *"arise with healing in his wings"* Mal. 4:2)*. **Come to know and love God our Father!**

Chapter 9

Galatians

*P*aul's letter to the Galatians contains seventeen passages that make a clear distinction between God and Jesus. They are:

1:1   "Paul, an apostle...by **Jesus** Christ, and **God** the Father, who raised him from the dead... ."

1:3   "Grace be to you and peace from **God** the Father, and from our Lord **Jesus** Christ... ."

1:4   "Who gave **himself** [Jesus] for our sins, that he might deliver us from this present evil world, according to the will of **God** and our Father... ."

1:10   "For do I now persuade men, or **God**? or do I seek to please men? for if I yet pleased men, I should not be the servant of **Christ**."

1:15-16   "But when it pleased **God**, who...called me by his grace, To reveal his **Son** [Jesus] in me... immediately I conferred not with flesh and blood... ."

1:22-24   "And [I] was unknown by face unto the churches of Judaea which were in **Christ**: But they had heard only, That he which persecuted us in times past now preacheth the faith which once he destroyed. And they glorified God in me."

2:17   "But if, while we seek to be justified by Christ, we ourselves also are found sinners, is therefore Christ the minister of sin? God forbid."

2:21   "I do not frustrate the grace of God: for if righteousness come by the law, then Christ is dead in vain."

3:17   "And this I say, that the covenant, that was confirmed before of God in Christ, the law, which was four hundred and thirty years after, cannot disannul... ."

3:21-22   "Is the law then against the promises of God? God forbid...But the scripture hath concluded all under sin, that the promise by faith of Jesus Christ might be given to them that believe."

3:26   "For ye are all the children of God by faith in Christ Jesus."

4:4   "But when the fulness of the time was come, God sent forth his Son, made of a woman... ."

4:6   "...God hath sent forth the Spirit of his Son into your hearts, crying, Abba, Father."

4:7   "...and if a son, then an heir of God through Christ."

4:14   "... but [ye] received me as an angel of God, even as
           Christ Jesus."

6:14   "But God forbid that I should glory, save in the cross
           of our Lord Jesus Christ... ."

6:16-17   "For in Christ Jesus neither circumcision availeth any
           thing, nor uncircumcision, but a new creature.
           And...peace be on them, and mercy, and upon the
           Israel of God."

Jesus' Greatest Lesson On Worship

*"Ye worship ye know not what: we know what we **worship**; for salvation is of the Jews. But the hour cometh, and now is, when the **true worshipers shall worship the Father** in spirit and in truth: for **the Father seeketh such to worship him**. God is a Spirit: And they that **worship him** must **worship him** in spirit and in truth. The woman saith unto him, I know that **Messiah** cometh, which is called Christ: when he is come, he will tell us all things. Jesus saith unto her, **I that speak unto thee am he**" (John 4:22-26).*

Question: Who authorized Christianity to disagree with Jesus on this most important subject?

Chapter 10

Ephesians

*P*aul's letter to the Ephesians contains thirty-one passages that make a clear distinction between God and Jesus. They are:

1:1   "Paul, an apostle of **Jesus** Christ by the will of **God**... ."

1:2   "Grace be to you, and peace, from **God** our Father, and from the Lord **Jesus** Christ."

1:3   "Blessed be the **God** and Father of our Lord **Jesus** Christ... ."

1:4   "According as **he** [God] hath chosen us in **him** [Jesus] before the foundation of the world... ."

1:5   "Having predestinated us unto the adoption of children by **Jesus** Christ to **himself** [God] according to the good pleasure of **his** [God's] will... ."

1:10   "That in the dispensation of the fulness of times **he** [God] might gather together in one all things in **Christ**, both which are in heaven, and which are on earth... ."

1:12   "That we should be to the praise of **his** [God's] glory, who first trusted in **Christ**."

93

1:17   "That the **God** of our Lord **Jesus** Christ, the Father of glory, may give unto you the spirit of wisdom and revelation in the knowledge of **him** [God]... ."

1:19-20   "And what is the exceeding greatness of **his** [God's] power...Which he wrought in **Christ**, when he raised him from the dead, and set him at **his** [God's] own right hand in the heavenly places... ."

2:4-5   "But **God**, who is rich in mercy...hath quickened us together with **Christ**... ."

2:7   "That in the ages to come **he** [God] might shew the exceeding riches of his grace in his kindness toward us through Christ **Jesus**."

2:10   "For we are **his** [God's] workmanship, created in Christ **Jesus** unto good works, which God hath before ordained that we should walk in them."

2:12   "That at that time ye were without **Christ**...having no hope, and without **God** in the world... ."

2:16   "And that **he** [Jesus] might reconcile both unto **God** in one body by the cross... ."

2:18   "For through **him** [Jesus] we both have access by one Spirit unto the **Father**."

2:19-20   "Now therefore ye are...of the household of **God**; And are built upon the foundation of the apostles and prophets, **Jesus** Christ himself being the chief corner stone... ."

2:22   "In **whom** [Jesus] ye also are builded together for an habitation of **God** through the Spirit."

3:1-2   "For this cause I Paul, the prisoner of **Jesus** Christ for you Gentiles, If ye have heard of the dispensation of the grace of **God** which is given me... ."

3-6   "That the Gentiles should be fellowheirs...and partakers of **his** [God's] promise in **Christ** by the gospel... ."

3:9   "And to make all men see what is the fellowship of the mystery, which from the beginning of the world hath been hid in **God**, who created all things by **Jesus** Christ."

3:10-11   "...the manifold wisdom of **God**, According to the eternal purpose which he purposed in Christ **Jesus** our Lord... ."

3:14   "For this cause I bow my knees unto the **Father** of our Lord **Jesus** Christ... ."

3:19   "And to know the love of **Christ**, which passeth knowledge, that ye might be filled with all the fullness of **God**."

3:21   "Unto **him** [God] be glory in the church by Christ **Jesus** throughout all ages, world without end. Amen."

4:5-6   "One **Lord** [Jesus] one faith, one baptism, One **God** and Father of all, who is above all, and through all, and in you all."

4:32   "...forgiving one another, even as **God** for **Christ's** sake hath forgiven you."

5:2   "And walk in love, as **Christ** also hath loved us, and hath given himself for us an offering and a sacrifice to **God**... ."

5:5   "For this ye know, that no whoremonger...hath any inheritance in the kingdom of **Christ** and of **God**."

5:20   "Giving thanks always for all things unto **God** and the Father in the name of our Lord **Jesus** Christ... ."

6:6   "Not with eyeservice, as menpleasers; but as the servants of **Christ**, doing the will of **God** from the heart... ."

6:23   "Peace be to the brethren...from **God** the Father and
        the Lord **Jesus** Christ".

Some Important Biblical Statistics

There are 31,000 verses in the Holy Bible and **not one** of these verses has the words "two" or "three" next to God.

Jesus spoke 1865 verses in the New Testament, and in **not one** of those verses did he claim (or even hint) that he is "God," a "second God," "God incarnate in flesh," or that he and God the Father are "one person."

The New Testament says *"God"* over 1300 times when it is clearly speaking of the **Father**, not Jesus.

Jesus said *"God"* 184 times and **not once** was he speaking of himself or the Holy Spirit, it was **always** the Father.

In the New Testament Jesus is called *"**Christ**"* 520 times, which means *"Messiah, the anointed one of God."*

Paul said *"God"* 513 times in his thirteen epistles and **not once** can it be proven that he was speaking of Jesus Messiah, it was **always** the Father.

Peter said *"God"* 46 times in his two epistles and **not once** was he referring to Jesus, it was **always** the Father.

James, the half brother of Jesus, said *"God"* 17 times in his epistle and **not once** was he referring to Jesus, it was **always** the Father. (Note: The focus of this book isn't who Jesus Christ is not, but who God the Father is).

Chapter 11

Philippians

*P*aul's letter to the Philippians contains eleven passages that make a clear distinction between God and Jesus. They are:

1:2   "Grace be unto you, and peace, from God our Father, and from the Lord Jesus Christ."

1:8   "For God is my record, how greatly I long after you all in the bowels of Jesus Christ."

1:11   "Being filled with the fruits of righteousness, which are by Jesus Christ, unto the glory and praise of God."

2:5-6   "Let this mind be in you, which was also in Christ Jesus...Who, being in the form [image] of God... ."

2:9   "Wherefore God also hath highly exalted him [Jesus], and given him a name which is above every name... ."

2:11   "And that every tongue should confess that Jesus Christ is Lord, to the glory of God the Father."

3:3   "For we are the circumcision, which worship God in the spirit, and rejoice in Christ Jesus... ."

3:9 "...that which is through the faith of Christ, the righteousness which is of God by faith...."

3:14 "I press toward the mark for the prize of the high calling of God in Christ Jesus."

4:7 "And the peace of God, which passeth all understanding, shall keep your hearts and minds through Christ Jesus."

4:19-20 "But my God shall supply all your need according to his riches in glory by Christ Jesus. Now unto God and our Father be glory for ever and ever."

Chapter 12

Colossians

*P*aul's letter to the Colossians contains sixteen passages that make a clear distinction between God and Jesus. They are:

1:1 "Paul, an apostle of Jesus Christ by the will of God... ."

1:2 "Grace be unto you, and peace, from God our Father and the Lord Jesus Christ."

1:3 "We give thanks to God and the Father of our Lord Jesus Christ, praying always for you... ."

1:10 "That ye might walk worthy of the Lord [Jesus] unto all pleasing, being fruitful in every good work, and increasing in the knowledge of God... ."

1:12-13 "Giving thanks unto the Father...Who hath delivered us from the power of darkness, and hath translated us into the kingdom of his dear Son... ."

1:15 "[Jesus] Who is the image of the invisible God, the firstborn of every creature... ."

1:19 "For it pleased the Father that in him [Jesus],should all fulness dwell... ." Note: Again, Christians are to *"be filled with all the fullness of God" (Eph. 3:19).*

101

1:27   "To whom **God** would make known what is the riches of the glory of this mystery among the Gentiles; which is **Christ** in you, the hope of glory... ."

2:2   "...to the acknowledgment of the mystery of **God**, and of the Father, and of **Christ**... ."

2:12   "Buried with **him** [Jesus] in baptism, wherein also ye are risen with him through the faith of the operation of **God**, who hath raised him from the dead."

3:1   "If ye then be risen with **Christ**, seek those things which are above, where Christ sitteth on the right hand of **God**."

3:3   "For ye are dead, and your life is hid with **Christ** in **God**."

3:16   "Let the word of **Christ** dwell in you richly in all wisdom; teaching and admonishing one another in psalms and hymns and spiritual songs, singing with grace in your hearts to the **Lord** [God]."   See Ephesians 5:20.

3:17   "And whatsoever ye do in word or deed, do all in the name of the Lord **Jesus**, giving thanks to **God** and the Father by him."

4:3 "Withal praying also for us, that **God** would open unto us a door of utterance, to speak the mystery of **Christ... .**"

4:12 "Epaphras, who is one of you, a servant of **Christ**...labouring fervently...that ye may stand perfect and complete in all the will of **God**".

John 5:44-45 (Jesus speaking):

*"You receive glory from one another and you do not seek the glory that is from the **one and only God...the father**"* (New American Standard Bible).

*"You don't seek the glory that comes from **the only God...the Father**"* (Holman CSB).

You..."care nothing for the honour that comes from **him who alone is God...the Father**" (The New English Bible).

You..."do not seek the glory that comes from **the only God...the Father**" (English Standard Version).

You..."make no effort to obtain the praise that comes from **the only God...the Father**" (New International Version).

*"You don't care about the honor that comes from **the one who alone is God...the Father**"* (New Living Translation).

You..."do not seek the honor that comes from **the only God...the Father**" (New King James Version).

Chapter 13

First Thessalonians

*P*aul's first letter to the Thessalonians contains fourteen passages that make a clear distinction between God and Jesus. They are:

1:1   "Paul...unto the church of the Thessalonians which is in God the Father and in the Lord Jesus Christ: Grace be unto you, and peace, from God our Father, and the Lord Jesus Christ."

1:3   "...hope in our Lord Jesus Christ, in the sight of God and our Father... ."

1:9 -10   "...and how ye turned to God from idols to serve the living and true God; And to wait for his Son from heaven, whom he raised from the dead, even Jesus, which delivered us from the wrath to come."

2:14   "For ye, brethren, became followers of the churches of God which in Judaea are in Christ Jesus... ."

2:15   "Who [the Jews] both killed the Lord Jesus...and they please not God... ."

3:2   "And [I] sent Timotheus, our brother, and minister of God, and our fellowlabourer in the gospel of Christ...".

3:11   "Now God himself and our Father, and our Lord Jesus Christ, direct our way unto you."

3:13   "To the end he may stablish your hearts unblameable in holiness before God, even our Father, at the coming of our Lord Jesus Christ with all his saints."

4:1   "Furthermore then we beseech you, brethren, and exhort you by the Lord Jesus, that as ye have received of us how ye ought to walk and to please God... ."

4:14   "...even so them also which sleep in Jesus will God bring with him."

4:16   "For the Lord himself shall descend from heaven with a shout, with the voice of the archangel, and with the trump of God: and the dead in Christ shall rise first... ."

5:9   "For God hath not appointed us to wrath, but to obtain salvation by our Lord Jesus Christ... ."

5:18   "In every thing give thanks: for this is the will of God in Christ Jesus concerning you."

5:23   "And the very **God** of peace sanctify you wholly; and I pray God your whole spirit and soul and body be preserved blameless unto the coming of our Lord **Jesus** Christ."

Jesus Himself Has A God

Jesus has a God whom he worships *(Ps. 18:49; John 4:22-23)*, whom he fears *(Isa. 11:1-5; Heb. 5:7)*; and to whom he prays *(Matt. 26:53; Luke 6:12, 22:44; Heb. 7:25)*. Notice these Scriptures regarding Jesus and his God.

> *"He shall stand and feed in the strength of the Lord, in the majesty of the name of **the Lord his God**" (Micah 5:4).*

> *"**My God, my God,** why hast thou forsaken me?" (Matt. 27:46).*

> *"I ascend unto...**my God**, and your God" (John 20:17).*

> *"Blessed be the **God** and Father of our Lord Jesus Christ. That the **God** of our Lord Jesus Christ, the Father of glory..." (Eph. 1:3, 17).*

> *"Blessed be the **God** and Father of our Lord Jesus Christ" (I Peter 1:3).*

> *"He that overcometh will I make a pillar in the temple of **my God**...name of **my God**...city of **my God**...down out of heaven from **my God**" (Rev. 3:12).*

This is the ascended Jesus speaking, who had been in heaven with the Father for some sixty years when the book of Revelation was written, but he still refers to God as *"my God."* It is for sure that Jesus cannot be the Supreme God, while he at the same time has a God to whom he submits.

Chapter 14

Second Thessalonians

*P*aul's second letter to the Thessalonians contains seven passages that make a clear distinction between God and Jesus. They are:

1:1   "Paul...unto the church of the Thessalonians in **God** our Father and the Lord Jesus **Christ**... ."

1:2   "Grace unto you, and peace, from **God** our Father and the Lord **Jesus** Christ."

1:8   "In flaming fire taking vengeance on them that know not **God**, and that obey not the gospel of our Lord **Jesus** Christ... ."

1:12   "...according to the grace of our **God** and the Lord **Jesus** Christ."

2:14   "Whereunto **he** ["God"] called you by our gospel, to the obtaining of the glory of our Lord **Jesus** Christ."

2:16-17 "Now our Lord **Jesus** Christ himself, and **God**, even our Father, which hath loved us...Comfort your hearts..... ."

3:5   "And the **Lord** direct your hearts into the love of **God**, and into the patient waiting for Christ."

Glory To God!

*"That ye may with one mind and one mouth **glorify God, even the Father** of our Lord Jesus Christ"* *(Rom. 15:6).*

*"To **God** only wise, **be glory through** Jesus Christ for ever" (Rom. 16:27).*

*"And I saw another angel fly in the midst of heaven...Saying with a loud voice, **Fear God, and give glory to him**" (Rev. 14:6-7).*

Note:

Glory - glorify (Greek - *"doxa"* - *"doxazo"* - Strong's #1391-92 *"To **recognize** a person or thing **for what it is**. It basically refers to the **recognition** belonging to a person - honor - renown. To **recognize**, honor, praise")* [1]

1. The Hebrew - Greek Study Bible; AMG International, Inc.; p. 1708-9.

Chapter 15

First Timothy

*P*aul's first letter to Timothy contains seven passages that make a clear distinction between God and Jesus. They are:

1:1   "Paul, an apostle of **Jesus** Christ by the commandment of **God**... ."

1:2   "...Grace, mercy, and peace, from **God** our Father and **Jesus** Christ our Lord."

1:16-17   "Howbeit for this cause I obtained mercy, that in me first **Jesus** Christ might shew forth all longsuffering...Now unto the King [God-the "great King"] eternal, immortal, invisible [Note: Jesus was not invisible-he was seen by thousands], the only wise **God**, be honour and glory for ever and ever. Amen."

2:5   "For there is one **God**, and one mediator between God and men, the man Christ **Jesus**... ."

4:5-6   For it (food) is sanctified by the word of **God** and prayer. If thou put the brethren in remembrance of these things, thou shalt be a good minister of **Jesus** Christ... ."

5:21   "I charge thee before **God**, and the Lord **Jesus** Christ, and the elect angels, that thou observe these things... ." [Note: No third person of a trinity is mentioned!]

6:13   "I give thee charge in the sight of **God**, who quickeneth all things, and before Christ **Jesus**... ."

Chapter 16

Second Timothy

*P*aul's second letter to Timothy contains eight passages that make a clear distinction between God and Jesus. They are:

1:1   "Paul, an apostle of **Jesus** Christ by the will of **God**... ."

1:2   "...Grace, mercy, and peace, from **God** the Father and Christ **Jesus** our Lord."

1:8   "Be not thou therefore ashamed of the testimony of our **Lord** [Jesus],...but be thou partaker of the afflictions of the gospel according to the power of **God**... ."

1:9   "[God] Who hath saved us, and called us with an holy calling...according to **his** (God's) own purpose and grace, which was given us in Christ **Jesus**... ."

2:8-9 "Remember that **Jesus** Christ...was raised from the dead according to my gospel: Wherein I suffer trouble...but the word of **God** is not bound."

2:19   "Nevertheless the foundation of **God** standeth sure... And, Let every one that nameth the name of **Christ** depart from iniquity."

3:15-16   "... from a child thou hast known the holy scriptures, which are able to make thee wise unto salvation through faith which is in Christ **Jesus**. All scripture is given by inspiration of **God**... ."

4:1   "I charge thee therefore before **God**, and the Lord **Jesus** Christ... ." Again no third person of a trinity is mentioned!

Chapter 17

Titus

*P*aul's letter to Titus contains three passages that make a clear distinction between God and Jesus. They are:

1:1 "Paul, a servant of God, and an apostle of Jesus Christ, according to the faith of God's elect... ."

1:4 "To Titus...Grace, mercy, and peace, from God the Father and the Lord Jesus Christ our Saviour."

2:13 "Looking for that blessed hope, and the glorious appearing of the great God and our Saviour Jesus Christ... ." Note: In due time God Himself is coming. See Matthew 5:8; 18:10; I Corinthians 15:21-28; Titus 2:13; Revelation 1:4-5, 8; 11:17; 16:5; 21:2-5; 22:1-6.

.

Paul Prayed To God

<u>Location of Prayer in Scripture</u><u>To Whom it was Addressed</u>

Location of Prayer in Scripture	To Whom it was Addressed
Acts 16:25	"God"
Acts 27:35	"God"
Acts 28:15	"God"
Romans 1:9-10	"God"
Romans 10:1	"God"
Romans 15:5-6	"God"
Romans 15:13	"God"
Romans 15:30	"God"
Romans 16:25-27	"God"
I Corinthians 1:4-9	"God"
II Corinthians 1:3-5	"God even the Father"
II Corinthians 2:14	"God"
II Corinthians 9:12-15	"God"
II Corinthians 13:7-9	"God"
Ephesians 1:15-23	"God"
Ephesians 3:14-21	"the Father of our Lord Jesus Christ"
Philippians 1:9-11	"God"
Philippians 4:20	"God our Father"
Colossians 1:9-12	"the Father" (God)
I Thessalonians 1:2-4	"God"
I Thessalonians 2:13	"God"
I Thessalonians 3:11-13	"God"
I Thessalonians 5:23-24	"God"
II Thessalonians 1:11-12	"God"
II Thessalonians 2:13-17	"God"
II Thessalonians 3:5	"the Lord...God"
II Thessalonians 3:16	"the Lord of peace"
I Timothy 1:17	"God"
I Timothy 6:13-17	"God" "whom no man hath seen"
II Timothy 1:3	"God"
II Timothy 1:16-18	"The Lord" (God)
II Timothy 4:14-18	"God"
Philemon 4-6	"God"

Chapter 18

Philemon

*P*aul's letter to Philemon contains one passage that makes a clear distinction between God and Jesus. It is:

1:3 "Grace to you, and peace, from **God** our Father and the Lord **Jesus** Christ."

Paul's View Of True Christian Worship

*"Speaking to yourselves in psalms and hymns and spiritual songs, singing and making melody in your heart to the Lord; Giving thanks **always** for **all things** unto **God and the Father** in the name of our Lord Jesus Christ"(Eph. 5:19-20).*

*"Let the word of Christ dwell in you richly as you teach and admonish one another with all wisdom, and as you sing psalms, hymns and spiritual songs with gratitude in your hearts **to God**. And whatever you do, whether in word or deed, do it all in the name of the Lord Jesus, **giving thanks to God the Father** through him" (Col. 3:16-17).*

*"For this cause I bow my knees **unto the Father** of our Lord Jesus Christ" (Ephesians 3:14).*

*"That ye may with one mind and one mouth **glorify God, even the Father** of our Lord Jesus Christ" (Romans 15:6).*

Chapter 19

Hebrews

T he book of Hebrews contains thirty-three passages that make a clear distinction between God and Jesus. They are:

1:1   "**God**, who....spake in time past unto the fathers...Hath in these last days spoken unto us by his **Son**, whom he hath appointed heir of all things... ."

1:3   "[Jesus] **Who** being the brightness of **his** [God's] glory, and the express image of his person..., sat down on the right hand of the Majesty [God] on high... ."

1:5   "Thou art my **Son**, this day have I begotten thee? And again, I will be to him a **Father**, and he shall be to me a Son?".

1:6   "And again, when he bringeth in the firstbegotten into the world, he saith, And let all the angels of **God** worship **him** [Jesus]."

1:8   "But unto the **Son** [Jesus] **he** [God] saith... ."

1:9   "**Thou** [Jesus] hast loved righteousness, and hated iniquity; therefore **God**, even thy God, hath anointed thee... ."

1:13   "...Sit on my right hand, until I [God] make **thine** [Jesus'] enemies thy footstool?"

2:3   "How shall we escape, if we neglect so great salvation; which at the first began to be spoken by the **Lord** [Jesus],and was confirmed unto us by them that heard him; **God** also bearing them witness...according to his own will?"

2:9   "But we see **Jesus**...crowned with glory and honour; that he by the grace of **God** should taste death for every man."

2:12   "Saying, I [Jesus] will declare **thy** [God's] name unto my brethren, in the midst of the church will I [Jesus] sing praise unto **thee** [God]."

2:13   "And again, Behold I [Jesus] and the children which **God** hath given me."

2:17   "Wherefore in all things it behoved **him** [Jesus] to be made like unto his brethren, that he might be a merciful and faithful high priest in things pertaining to **God**... ."

3:1-2   "Wherefore, holy brethren...consider the Apostle and High Priest of our profession, Christ **Jesus**; Who was faithful to **him** [God] that appointed him... ."

4:14   "Seeing then that we have a great high priest, that is passed into the heavens, **Jesus** the Son of **God**.."

5:5   "So also **Christ** glorified not himself to be made an high priest; but **he** [God] that said unto him, Thou art my Son, to day have I begotten thee."

5:6   "As **he** [God] saith also in another place, **Thou** [Jesus] art a priest for ever ... ."

5:7   "Who in the days of **his** [Jesus'] flesh, when he had offered up prayers and supplications with strong crying and tears unto **him** [God] that was able to save him from death, and was heard in that he feared... ."

5:8-10   "Though he [Jesus] were a **Son**, yet learned he obedience by the things which he suffered; And being made perfect, he became the author of eternal salvation unto all them that obey him; Called of **God** an high priest ... ."

6:1   "Therefore leaving the principles of the doctrine of **Christ**, let us go on unto perfection; not laying again the foundation of repentance from dead works, and of faith toward **God**... ."

7:21-22   "(For those priests were made without an oath; but this with an oath by **him** [God] that said unto **him** [Jesus], The **Lord** [God] sware and will not repent, Thou art a priest for ever after the order of Melchisedec:) By so much was **Jesus** made a surety of a better testament ."

7:25   "Wherefore **he** [Jesus] is able also to save them to the uttermost that come unto **God** by him... ."

8:1   "...We have such an **high priest** [Jesus], who is set on the right hand of the throne of the **Majesty** [God] in the heavens... ."

9:14   "How much more shall the blood of **Christ**, who through the eternal Spirit offered himself without spot to **God**, purge your conscience from dead works to serve the living God?"

9:24   "For **Christ** is not entered into the holy places made with hands...but into heaven itself, now to appear in the presence of **God** for us... ."

10:7   "Then said **I** [Jesus], Lo, I come (in the volume of the book it is written of me,) to do thy will, O **God**."

10:9   "Then said **he** [Jesus], Lo, I come to do thy will, O **God**."

10:12-13   "But this **man** [Jesus], after he had offered one sacrifice for sins for ever, sat down on the right hand of **God**; From henceforth expecting till his enemies be made his footstool."

10:21   "And having an **high priest** [Jesus] over the house of **God**; Let us draw near with a true heart... ."

11:25-26   "Choosing rather to suffer affliction with the people of **God**, than to enjoy the pleasures of sin for a season; Esteeming the reproach of **Christ**... ."

12:2   "Looking unto **Jesus** the author and finisher of our faith; who...is set down at the right hand of the throne of **God**."

12:22-24   "But ye are come unto mount Sion... and to **God** the Judge of all...And to **Jesus** the mediator of the new covenant... ."

13:15-16   "By **him** [Jesus] therefore let us offer the sacrifice of praise to **God** continually...for with such sacrifices God is well pleased."

13:20-21   "Now the **God** of peace, that brought again from the dead our Lord **Jesus**...Make you perfect... ."

Who Was Jesus Thanking?

*"And he took the cup and **gave thanks**" (Luke 22:17).*

*"...and he took the seven loaves, and **gave thanks**" (Mark 8:6).*

*"And he took the cup and when he had **given thanks**" (Mark 14:23).*

*"And he took bread and **gave thanks**" (Luke 22:19).*

*"...nigh unto the place where they did eat bread, after that the **Lord** had **given thanks**" (John 6:23).*

Chapter 20

James

T he book of James contains one passage that makes a clear distinction between God and Jesus. It is:

1:1   "James, a servant of God and of the Lord Jesus Christ, to the twelve tribes which are scattered abroad, greeting."

Note: James says "God" seventeen times in his small but powerful book and not once is he speaking of Jesus, it is always the Father! For example:

1:13   "...for God cannot be tempted with evil... ."

1:17   "Every good gift and every perfect gift is from above, and cometh down from the Father... ."

2:27   "Pure religion and undefiled before God and the Father is this, To visit the fatherless and widows in their affliction... ."

2:19   "Thou believest that there is one God; thou doest well: the devils also believe, and tremble."

A Statement Of Truth

"Today, however, scholars generally agree that there is no doctrine of the Trinity as such in either the Old Testament or the New Testament...It would go far beyond the intention and thought-forms of the Old Testament to suppose that a late-forth-century or thirteenth-century Christian doctrine can be found there...Likewise, the New Testament does not contain an explicit doctrine of the Trinity."

The Harper Collins Encyclopedia of

Catholicism;1995 Edition; p. 564-565

Chapter 21

First Peter

*T*he book of First Peter contains eighteen passages that make a clear distinction between God and Jesus. They are:

1:2   "Elect according to the foreknowledge of **God** the Father...unto obedience and sprinkling of the blood of **Jesus** Christ... ."

1:3   "Blessed be the **God** and Father of our Lord **Jesus** Christ... ."

1:17-19   "And if ye call on the **Father**...Forasmuch as ye know that ye were not redeemed with corruptible things, as silver and gold...But with the precious blood of **Christ**... ."

1:21   "Who by **him** [Jesus] do believe in **God**, that raised him up from the dead, and gave him glory; that your faith and hope might be in **God**."

2:4   "To **whom** [Jesus] coming, as unto a living stone, disallowed indeed of men, but chosen of **God**, and precious... ."

2:5   "Ye also, as lively stones, are built up a spiritual house, an holy priesthood, to offer up spiritual sacrifices, acceptable to **God** by **Jesus** Christ."

2:6   "...Behold, **I** [God] lay in Sion a **chief corner stone** [Jesus],elect, precious: and he that believeth on him shall not be confounded."

2:20-21   "...if, when ye do well, and suffer for it, ye take it patiently, this is acceptable with **God**. For even hereunto were ye called: because **Christ** also suffered for us... ."

2:23   "Who, when **he** [Jesus] was reviled, reviled not again; when he suffered, he threatened not; but committed himself to **him** [God] that judgeth righteously... ."

3:15-16   "But sanctify the **Lord God** in your hearts...Having a good conscience; that...they may be ashamed that falsely accuse your good conversation in **Christ**."

3:18   "For **Christ** also hath once suffered for sins, the just for the unjust, that he might bring us to **God**... ."

3:21   "...(not the putting away of the filth of the flesh, but the answer of a good conscience toward **God**,) by the resurrection of **Jesus** Christ... ."

3:22   "[Jesus] **Who** is gone into heaven, and is on the right hand of **God**; angels and authorities and powers being made subject unto **him** [Jesus]."

4:1-2   "Forasmuch then as **Christ** hath suffered for us in the flesh, arm yourselves likewise with the same mind...to the will of **God**."

4:11   "If any man speak, let him speak as the oracles of **God**; if any man minister, let him do it as of the ability which God giveth: that God in all things may be glorified through **Jesus** Christ... ."

4:14   "If ye be reproached for the name of **Christ**, happy are ye; for the spirit of glory and of **God** resteth upon you... ."

5:1-2   "The elders which are among you I exhort, who am also an elder, and a witness of the sufferings of **Christ**...Feed the flock of **God** which is among you... ."

5:10   "But the **God** of all grace, who hath called us unto his eternal glory by Christ **Jesus**, after that ye have suffered a while, make you perfect, stablish, strengthen, settle you."

Peter's Confession

Question: What was Peter's confession upon which Jesus said *"I will build my Church?"*

> *"Thou art the* **Christ***, the Son of the living God" (Matthew 16:16).*

> *"Thou art the* **Christ***" (Mark 8:29).*

> *"The* **Christ** *of God" (Luke 9:20).*

The sad fact is that most of Christianity has built its churches on the mistaken confession that Jesus is "God," "God the Son," or the "second person of a triune God." Peter would not recognize nor endorse these confessions!

Chapter 22

Second Peter

*T*he book of Second Peter contains four passages that make a clear distinction between God and Jesus. They are:

1:1   "Simon Peter, a servant and an apostle of **Jesus** Christ...through the righteousness of **God** and our Saviour Jesus Christ... ."

1:2   "Grace and peace be multiplied unto you through the knowledge of **God**, and of **Jesus** our Lord... ."

1:17   "For **he** [Jesus] received from **God** the Father honour and glory, when there came such a voice to him from the excellent glory, This is my beloved **Son**, in whom **I** [God] am well pleased."

1:18   "And this **voice** [God's] which came from heaven we heard, when we were with **him** [Jesus] in the holy mount."

*"Our opponents sometime claim that no belief should be held dogmatically which is not explicitly stated in Scripture...but the **Protestant churches** have themselves accepted such dogmas as **the Trinity**, for which there is **no such precise authority** in the Gospels."*

Noted Catholic scholar Graham Greene

Defending the dogma of the Assumption of Mary.

Chapter 23

First John

*T*he book of First John contains nineteen passages that make a clear distinction between God and Jesus. They are:

1:3   "... and truly our fellowship is with the **Father**, and with his Son **Jesus** Christ."

1-5-7   "...**God** is light, and in him is no darkness ...But if we walk in the light, as he [God] is in the light, we have fellowship one with another, and the blood of **Jesus** Christ his Son cleanseth us from all sin."

2:1   "And if any man sin, we have an advocate with the **Father**, **Jesus** Christ the righteous...."

2:22   "...He is antichrist, that denieth the **Father** and the **Son**."

2:23   "Whosoever denieth the **Son**, the same hath not the **Father**... ."

2:24   "If that which ye have heard from the beginning shall remain in you, ye also shall continue in the **Son**, and in the **Father**."

3:8-9   "For this purpose the **Son** of God was manifested, that he might destroy the works of the devil. Whosoever is born of **God** doth not commit sin...because he is born of God."

3:23   "And this is **his** [God's] commandment, That we should believe on the name of his [God's] Son **Jesus** Christ... ."

4:2   "Hereby know ye the Spirit of **God**: Every spirit that confesseth that **Jesus** Christ is come in the flesh is of God... ."

4:3   "And every spirit that confesseth not that **Jesus** Christ is come in the flesh is not of **God**... ."

4:9   "In this was manifested the love of **God** toward us, because that God sent his only begotten **Son** into the world... ."

4:10   "Herein is love, not that we loved **God**, but that he loved us, and sent his **Son** to be the propitiation for our sins."

4:14   "And we have seen and do testify that the **Father** sent the **Son** to be the Saviour of the world. Whosoever shall confess that **Jesus** is the Son of **God**, God dwelleth in him, and he in God."

5:1   "Whosoever believeth that **Jesus** is the Christ is born of **God**... ."

5:5   "Who is he that overcometh the world, but he that believeth that **Jesus** is the Son of **God**?"

5:9   "If we receive the witness of men, the witness of **God** is greater: for this is the witness of God which he hath testified of his **Son**."

5:10   "...he that believeth not **God** hath made him a liar; because he believeth not the record that God gave of his **Son**."

5:11   "And this is the record, that **God** hath given to us eternal life, and this life is in his **Son**."

5:20   "And we know that the Son of God is come, and hath given us an understanding, that we may know **him** [God] that is true, and we are in **him** [God] that is true, even in his [God's] Son **Jesus** Christ."

What Must We Believe About Jesus To Be Saved?

Question: According to Holy Scripture, what **belief about Jesus** is required for salvation?

Listen to Simon Peter:
"Thou art the Christ [Messiah], *the **Son** of the living God"* *(Matt. 16:16)*. Note: Not *"the living God,"* but *"the **Son** of the living God!"*

Listen to the apostle John as to why he wrote his Gospel:
"But these [truths] *are written, that ye might believe that Jesus is the Christ* [Messiah] *the **Son of God**; and that **believing** ye might have life through his name" (John 20:31)*. Again, not *"God,"* but, *"Messiah, the **Son** of God!"*

Listen to the eunuch's confession before baptism by Philip:
*"I **believe** that Jesus Christ is **the Son of God**" (Acts 8:37)*.

Listen to Paul's first sermon after his Damascus road encounter with Jesus:
*"And straightway he preached Christ in the synagogues, that he is **the Son of God**" (Acts 9:20)*.

Listen to Jesus' declaration made some 60 years after his ascension to the Father:
*"These things saith **the Son of God**" (Rev. 2:18)*. Notice carefully: Not *"God,"* or *"God the Son!"*

In John 20:31 above, the apostle makes an awesome promise to those who believe that *"**Jesus is the Messiah, the Son of God.**"* That promise is eternal *"life!"* Here are more such promises from John.

*"Whosoever shall **confess** that Jesus is **the Son of God, God dwelleth in him**, and he in God" (I John 4:15)*.

*"Whosoever **believeth** that **Jesus is the Messiah is born of God**" (I John 5:1)*.

*"Who is **he that overcometh the world**, but he that **believeth** that Jesus is **the Son of God**" (I John 5:5)*.

*"...that ye may know that ye have **eternal life**, and that ye may **believe** on the name of **the Son of God**" (I John 5:13)*.

Where are the promises made to those who believe that Jesus is *"God," "God the Son,"* or *"the second person of the Trinity?"* **They cannot be found!**

Chapter 24

Second John

*T*he book of Second John contains two passages that make a clear distinction between God and Jesus. They are:

1:3   "Grace be with you, mercy, and peace, from **God** the Father, and from the Lord **Jesus** Christ, the **Son** of the **Father**, in truth and love."

1:9   "Whosoever transgresseth, and abideth not in the doctrine of **Christ**, hath not **God**. He that abideth in the doctrine of Christ, he hath both the **Father** and the **Son**."

God Did Not Become A Man!

There is not one verse in the Bible that says God needed to, intended to, or did become a man!

*"For **I am God**, and **not man**; the **Holy One** in the midst of thee" (Hosea 11:9).*

*"**God is not a man**....neither the son of man...." (Num. 23:19).*

"For he (God) *is not a man...." (I Sam. 15:29).*

The eternal God has a human Son who is a man!

*"Ye seek to kill me, **a man** that has told you the truth, **which I have heard of God***" (Jesus speaking) *(John 8:40).*

*"Greater love hath no **man** than this, that **a man** lay down his life for his friends. Ye are my friends...."* (Jesus speaking) *(John 15:13-14).*

*"If I had not done among them the works which **none other man** did....* (Jesus speaking) *(John 15:24).*

*"For there is **one God**, and one mediator between **God** and **men**, the **man Christ Jesus**" (I Tim. 2:5).*

Note: Jesus is called "son of man" 84 times in the Gospels. God called Ezekiel "son of man" 90 times in the book of Ezekiel. It means **a human being**.

Chapter 25

Jude

T he book of Jude contains three passages that make a clear distinction between God and Jesus. They are:

1:1   "Jude...to them that are sanctified by **God** the Father, and preserved in **Jesus** Christ... ."

1:4   "For there are certain men crept in unawares...turning the grace of our God into lasciviousness, and denying the only **Lord God**, and our Lord **Jesus** Christ."

1:21   "Keep yourselves in the love of **God**, looking for the mercy of our Lord **Jesus** Christ unto eternal life."

"It is fair to say that the Bible does not clearly teach the doctrine of the Trinity, if by clearly one means there are proof texts for the doctrine. In fact, there is not even one proof text, if by proof text we mean a verse or passage that 'clearly' states that there is one God who exists in three persons" (p. 89). *"The above illustrations prove the fallacy of concluding that if something is not proof texted in the Bible we cannot clearly teach the results... . If that were so, I could never teach the doctrines of the Trinity or the deity of Christ or the deity of the Holy Spirit"* (p. 90).

(Trinitarian scholar Charles C Ryrie; *Basic Theology*)

Chapter 26

Revelation

$\mathcal{T}$ he book of Revelation contains forty passages that make a clear distinction between God and Jesus. They are:

1:1   "The Revelation of Jesus Christ, which God gave unto him...".

1:2   "[John] Who bare record of the word of God, and of the testimony of Jesus Christ, and of all things that he saw."

1:4-5   "...Grace be unto you, and peace, from him [God] which is, and which was, and which is to come; and from the seven Spirits which are before his [God's] throne; And from Jesus Christ... ." Note: Now with this understanding please study carefully verse eight of chapter one.

1:6   "And hath made us kings and priests unto God and his [Jesus'] Father; to him be glory and dominion for ever and ever. Amen."

1:9   "I John...was in the isle that is called Patmos, for the word of God, and for the testimony of Jesus Christ."

2:7   "...To him that overcometh will I [Jesus] give to eat of the tree of life, which is in the midst of the paradise of **God**."

2:26-27   "And he that overcometh, and keepeth **my** [Jesus'] works unto the end, to him will I give power over the nations...even as I received of my **Father**."

3:2   "...I [Jesus] have not found thy works perfect before **God**."

3:5   "He that overcometh...I [Jesus] will confess his name before my **Father**, and before his angels."

3:12   "Him that overcometh will I [Jesus] make a pillar in the temple of my **God**...and I [Jesus] will write upon him the name of my **God**, and the name of the city of my **God**, which is new Jerusalem, which cometh down out of heaven from my **God**: and I [Jesus] will write upon him my new name."

3:14   "...These things saith the **Amen** [Jesus], the faithful and true witness [Jesus], the beginning of the creation of **God**... ."

3:21   "To him that overcometh will I [Jesus] grant to sit with me in my throne, even as I [Jesus] also overcame, and am set down with my **Father** in his throne."

5:6   "And I beheld, and, lo...in the midst of the elders, stood a **Lamb** [Jesus] as it had been slain, having seven horns and seven eyes, which are the seven Spirits of **God**... ."

5:7   "And **he** [Jesus] came and took the book out of the right hand of **him** [God] that sat upon the throne."

5:9-10   "And they sung a new song, saying, **Thou** [Jesus] art worthy to take the book, and to open the seals thereof: for thou [Jesus] wast slain, and hast redeemed us to **God** ...And hast made us unto our God kings and priests... ."

5:13   "And every creature...heard I saying, Blessing, and honour, and glory, and power, be unto **him** [God] that sitteth upon the throne, and unto the **Lamb** [Jesus] for ever and ever."

6:16   "...Fall on us, and hide us from the face of **him** [God] that sitteth on the throne, and from the wrath of the **Lamb**..." .

7:10   "...Salvation to our **God** which sitteth upon the throne, and unto the **Lamb**."

7:17   "For the **Lamb** which is in the midst of the throne shall feed them...and **God** shall wipe away all tears from their eyes."

11:15   "...The kingdoms of this world are become the kingdoms of our **Lord** [God], and of his **Christ**... ."

12:5   "And she brought forth a man **child** [Jesus], who was to rule all nations with a rod of iron: and her child was caught up unto **God**, and to his throne."

12:10   "And I heard a loud voice saying in heaven, Now is come salvation, and strength, and the kingdom of our **God**, and the power of his **Christ**... ."

12:17   "And the dragon was wroth with the woman, and went to make war with the remnant of her seed, which keep the commandments of **God**, and have the testimony of **Jesus** Christ."

14:1   "And I looked, and, lo, a **Lamb** [Jesus] stood on the mount Sion, and with him an hundred forty and four thousand, having his **Father's** name written in their foreheads."

14:4   "These were redeemed from among men, being the firstfruits unto **God** and to the **Lamb** [Jesus]."

14:10   "The same shall drink of the wine of the wrath of **God**...in the presence of the holy angels, and in the presence of the **Lamb** [Jesus]... ."

14:12   "... here are they that keep the commandments of **God**, and the faith of **Jesus**."

15:3   "And they sing the song of Moses the servant of **God**, and the song of the **Lamb**, saying, Great and marvellous are thy works, Lord **God** Almighty... ."

19:6-7   "...the Lord **God** omnipotent reigneth. Let us be glad and rejoice, and give honour to him [God] for the marriage of the **Lamb** is come... ."

19:9   "And he saith unto me, Write, Blessed are they which are called unto the marriage supper of the **Lamb**. And he saith unto me, These are the true sayings of **God**."

19:10   "...I am thy fellowservant, and of thy brethren that have the testimony of **Jesus**: worship **God**... ."

19:15   "...and **he** [Jesus] treadeth the winepress of the fierceness and wrath of Almighty **God**."

20:4   "...and I saw the souls of them that were beheaded for the witness of **Jesus**, and for the word of **God**...and they lived and reigned with Christ a thousand years."

20:6   "...they shall be priests of **God** and of **Christ**, and shall reign with him [Christ Jesus] a thousand years."

21:10,11,14"And he...shewed me that great city, the holy Jerusalem, descending out of heaven from God, Having the glory of **God**...And the wall of the city had twelve foundations, and in them the names of the twelve apostles of the Lamb [Jesus]."

21:22 "And I saw no temple therein: for the Lord God Almighty and the Lamb [Jesus] are the temple of it."

21:23 "And the city had no need of the sun, neither of the moon, to shine in it: for the glory of God did lighten it, and the Lamb is the light [Greek-luchnos-"lamp"] thereof."

22:1 "And he shewed me a pure river of water of life, clear as crystal, proceeding out of the throne of God and of the Lamb."

22:3-4 "And there shall be no more curse: but the throne of God and of the Lamb shall be in it; and his [God's] servants shall serve him: and they shall see his [God's] face [see Matt.5:8]; and his [God the Father's] name shall be in their foreheads [see Rev. 14:1]."

22:19 "And if any man shall take away from the words of the book of this prophecy, God shall take away his part out of the book of life...He [Jesus] which testifieth these things saith, Surely I come quickly. Amen. Even so, come, Lord Jesus."

To God be the glory!

Chapter 27

The God Of The Bible Is One-Not Three

> *"For the weapons of our warfare are not carnal,*
> *but mighty through God to the pulling down of*
> *strong holds; Casting down imaginations, and*
> *every high thing that exalteth itself against the*
> *knowledge of God, and bringing into captivity*
> *every thought to the obedience of Christ..."(2*
> *Corinthians 10:4, 5).*

*T*he verses above present the greatest of all challenges to Christianity today! Casting down imaginations (i.e. speculations) and every "high thing" that would exalt itself against the true **knowledge of God**, and bringing into captivity every *"thought"* (Greek - noema--perception, belief) to obedience to the teachings of Christ. Today's English Version translates this passage very well.

> *"We destroy false arguments; we pull down*
> *every proud obstacle that is raised against **the***
> ***knowledge of God**; we take every thought*
> *captive and make it **obey Christ**" (2 Cor. 10:4-5*
> *Today's English Version).*

We make every belief about God come into obedience to the teachings of Christ! Jesus came to teach us **about God**, and to bring us **to God**. He denied being God *(Matt. 19:17; John*

5:19,30-32; 7:16-17). He said the greatest commandment is, *"Listen...God is **one Lord"** (Mark 12:29-30)*. He said the Father is *"the only true God" (John 17:3)*. He said, I do not know when I am coming back to earth, only my Father knows *(Mark 13:32)*. He said that in his own future kingdom, *"to sit on my right hand, and on my left, **is not mine to give**, but it shall be given to them for whom it is prepared of **my Father"** (Matt. 20:23)*. He said, *"I ascend **unto my Father**, and your Father; and **to my God**, and your God" (John 20:17)*. He said God our Father has a *"face" (Matt. 18:10)*. He said, to a multitude who were blessed to see him, the pure in heart *"shall see **God"** (Matt. 5:8)*. Seven times he spoke of *"my Father which is in heaven,"* and nine times, *"your Father which is in heaven."* And there is so much more!

On the Mall in Washington, D.C., a thirty foot monument was recently dedicated to the memory of Martin Luther King, Jr., the founder of the Civil Rights movement. In the beautiful white granite are carved excerpts from his statements and speeches that reflect his views on which the movement was founded. However, after its erection, some of his supporters, people whose lives have been touched by his teachings, life, and death, noticed that one of the statements misquoted Dr. King. They were incensed because the misquote made him appear to have been prideful and egotistical, which he was not! After considerable protest from these friends, the misrepresentation was removed from the memorial.

The lesson in the above for Christianity is this, the views of Jesus Christ, the founder of the Christian religion, regarding the most

148

important subject in the world, Who is God?, have been distorted beyond recognition, and every lover and follower of Jesus should be incensed! As an example of how orthodox Christian doctrine differs from his, I have a standing offer of $10,000.00 for any verse in the KJV Bible where Jesus claimed to be "God," "God the Son," or made one statement regarding a "Trinity." There have been no takers! Jesus taught that God is *"one"* entity, being, person, *(Mark 12:29-34)*, and Christianity teaches that God is *three persons*. He said we should give our *God worship* to the *"Father,"* and *"him only" (John 4:23; Luke 4:8)*, and Christianity worships *"the **man** Messiah Jesus"* as God! He claimed to be *"a **man** that hath told you the truth, which I have heard of [from] **God**" (John 8:40)*. To those who accused him of making himself "God" he replied, *"I said, I am the Son of God" (John 10: 32-36)*. Note: They never mentioned the "God" thing again! Christianity makes Jesus "God," although when he himself said "God" one hundred-eighty-four times as recorded in the N.T., not once was he speaking of himself, it was always the **Father**!

The Man Christ Jesus

Jesus' favorite name for himself while on earth, which he used over eighty times as recorded in the Gospels, was *"the Son of man."* This is the same term by which God addressed Ezekiel some ninety times in the book that bears his name, and it means **a human being**. This word "man" that Jesus used is **anthropos in the Greek** *(Strong's #444)*, and again it has only one meaning, *"a human being!"* Note: Jesus often referred to himself coming back to earth as *"the Son of man."*

We as Christians must come into agreement with our Lord Jesus Messiah regarding these awesome truths about God. Only then will we be *"unto God a sweet aroma of Christ" (II Cor. 2:15)*, and remove the smell of Plato from our garments! (See my book, *Glory To God In The Highest - Removing The Influence of Socrates, Plato, and Philo from Christian Doctrine).* Only then will we "increase in favor with God" as Jesus did *(Luke 2:52)*, so that we might have signs, wonders, miracles, and Apostolic power for the end-time as God has promised *(Daniel 11:32; John 14:12).*

A question for Christianity--If God is with us...?

In Judges chapter six the story is told of Israel's oppression by their enemies, and the consequences of their backsliding are described.

> *"And they encamped against them, and destroyed the increase of the earth...and left no sustenance for Israel, neither sheep, nor ox, nor ass. And Israel was greatly impoverished because of the Midianites; and the children of Israel cried unto The Lord" (Judges 6:4, 6).*

God heard their cries and sent an angel to visit an Israelite man named Gideon who was in hiding, threshing his wheat.

> *"And the angel of the Lord appeared unto him, and said unto him,* **The Lord is with thee***, thou mighty man of valor" (v. 12).*

To this Gideon responded with a question!

> *"And Gideon said unto him, Oh my Lord, if the Lord be with us, why then is all this befallen us?*

150

and where be all his miracles which our fathers told us of..." (v. 13).

Where are the miracles which *our* fathers (the Apostles) told us of? Today Christianity is anemic, divided, and powerless! Jesus pictured a different Christianity!

> *"Verily, verily, I say unto you, He that believeth on me, the works that I do shall he do also; and greater works than these shall he do; because I go unto my Father" (John 14:12).*

> *"And these signs shall follow them that believe; In my name shall they cast out devils; they shall speak with new tongues; They shall take up serpents; and if they drink any deadly thing, it shall not hurt them; they shall lay hands on the sick, and they shall recover. So then after the Lord had spoken unto them, he was received up into heaven, and sat on the right hand of God. And they went forth, and preached every where, the Lord working with them, and confirming the word with signs following. Amen" (Mark 16:17-20).*

Perhaps this is the answer

> *"Whosoever transgresseth, **and abideth not in the doctrine of Christ**, hath not God. He that abideth in the doctrine of Christ, he hath both the Father and the Son" (II John 1:9 KJV).*

151

> *"Anyone who **runs ahead and does not continue in the teaching of Christ** does not have God" (II John 1:9 NIV).*

> *"If anybody does not **keep within the teaching of Christ but goes beyond it**, he cannot have God with him" (II John 1:9 Jerusalem Bible).*

As it is often said today, go figure!

God is not a man!

There is not one verse in the Holy Bible, Old or New Testament, where God the Creator ever said He wanted to be a man, needed to be a man, intended to be a man, or would gain anything for us or Himself by becoming a man! In fact He states clearly that He is not a man.

> *"For I am God, and not man; the Holy One in the midst of thee" (Hosea 11:9).*

> *"God is not a man...neither the son of man" (Numbers 23:19).*

> *"And also the Strength of Israel...he is not a man" (I Samuel 15:29).*
> *"For he (God) is not a man..." (Job 9:32).*

So why do Christian ministers keep saying, "God became a man?"

God Is One!

In total agreement with the teachings of Jesus, the God declared in the entire Bible is **one** *entity, being, person.* Moses gave Israel their everlasting creed in Deuteronomy 6:4, "God is **one** Lord." The apostle James said, " there is **one** God," and the apostle Paul said, "there is none other God but **one**...there is but **one** God, the Father" *(I Cor. 8:4,6).* The last page of the Bible pictures **one** God, and one Lamb of God *(Rev. 22:1, 3).* Every other verse of Scripture agrees with these foundational statements of truth. In fact, there are 31,000 verses in the Bible, and not one Holy Spirit inspired verse ever had the word "three" next to God. (Note: I John 5:7, *"and these three are one,"* has been proven by scholars to be a forgery, inserted after 1500 A.D. by someone determined to have at least one trinitarian verse in the Holy Bible. See proof at the end of this chapter).

The following sixty-five verses, many spoken by God Himself, and all inspired by Him, prove beyond a shadow of a doubt that God is **one** - not three! As you read these verses please keep in mind what God says regarding Abraham in Ezekiel 33:24, *"Abraham was* ***one,"*** and ask yourself if Abraham was three persons or one person. What is so hard to understand about the word *"one?"* Please agree with me that one is one--is one.

Sixty-five verses of Scripture.

"Hear, O Israel: The Lord our God is one Lord" (Deut. 6:4).

"...did not one fashion us in the womb" (Job 31:15)?

"O my God...thou Holy One of Israel" (Psalm 71:22).

"...and tempted God and limited the Holy One of Israel" (Psalm 78:41).

"...the Holy One of Israel is our king" (Psalm 89:18).

"...they have provoked the Holy One of Israel" (Isaiah 1:4).

"...the Lord of hosts, the mighty One of Israel" (Isaiah 1:24).

"...the counsel of the Holy One of Israel" (Isaiah 5:19).

"...the word of the Holy One of Israel" (Isaiah 5:24).

"...the Lord, the Holy One of Israel" (Isaiah 10:20).

"...great is the Holy One of Israel" (Isaiah 12:6).

"...respect to the Holy One of Israel" (Isaiah 17:7).

*"...rejoice in the Holy **One** of Israel" (Isaiah 29:19).*

*"...the Holy **One** of Jacob...the **God** of Israel" (Isaiah 29:23).*

*"...the Holy **One** of Israel" (Isaiah 30:11).*

*"...thus saith the Holy **One** of Israel" (Isaiah 30:12).*

*"For thus saith the **Lord God**, the Holy **One** of Israel" (Isaiah 30:15).*

*"...the mighty **One** of Israel" (Isaiah 30:29).*

*"...they look not unto the Holy **One** of Israel" (Isaiah 31:1).*

*"...the Holy **One** of Israel" (Isaiah 37:23).*

*"To whom will ye liken me...saith the Holy **One**" (Isaiah 40:25)?*

*"...thy Redeemer, the Holy **One** of Israel" (Isaiah 41:14).*

*"...shalt glory in the Holy **One** of Israel" (Isaiah 41:17).*

*"...the Holy **One** of Israel hath created it"* *(Isaiah 41:20)*.

*"I am the Lord thy **God**, the Holy **One** of Israel"* *(Isaiah 43:3)*.

*"...your redeemer, the Holy **One** of Israel"* *(Isaiah 43:14)*.

*"I am the Lord, your Holy **One**, the creator of Israel, your King" (Isaiah 43:15)*.

*"...the Lord of hosts is his name, the Holy **One** of Israel" (Isaiah 47:4)*.

*"...the Holy **One** of Israel; I am the Lord thy **God**" (Isaiah 48:17)*.

*"...the Redeemer of Israel, and his Holy **One**"* *(Isaiah 49:7)*.

*"...the Lord that is faithful, and the Holy **One** of Israel" (Isaiah 49:7)*.

*"...all flesh shall know that I the Lord am thy Savior and thy Redeemer, the mighty **One** of Jacob" (Isaiah 49:26)*.

"For thy Maker...the Holy One of Israel; The God of the whole earth" (Isaiah 54:5).

"...the Lord thy God, and for the Holy One of Israel" (Isaiah 55:5).

"For thus saith the high and lofty One that inhabiteth eternity" (Isaiah 57:15).

"...the Lord thy God, and to the Holy One of Israel" (Isaiah 60:9).

"The Zion of the Holy One of Israel" (Isaiah 60:14).

"...thy Redeemer, the mighty One of Jacob" (Isaiah 60:16).

"...against the Holy One of Israel" (Jeremiah 50:29).

"...God, the Lord of hosts...the Holy One of Israel" (Jeremiah 51:5).

"...and I heard a voice of one that spoke...Thus saith the Lord God" (Ezekiel 1:28; 2:4).

"...the heathen shall know that I am the Lord, the Holy One in Israel. ...saith the Lord God" (Ezekiel 39:7-8).

"I am God, and not man; the Holy One" (Hosea 11:9).

"O Lord my God, mine Holy One...O mighty God" (Habakkuk 1:12).

"God came from Teman, and the Holy One from mount Paran" (Habakkuk 3:3).

"...in that day shall there be one Lord and his name one" (Zechariah 14:9).

"Have we not all one father? Hath not one God created us" (Malachi 2:10)?

"Why callest thou me good? There is none good but one, that is God" [Jesus speaking] *(Matthew 19:17).*

"...one is your Father, which is in heaven...one is your Master, even Christ" [Jesus speaking] *(Matthew 23:9-10).*

"...there is none good but one, that is God" (Mark 10:18).

*"The Lord our **God** is **one** Lord"* [Jesus speaking] *(Mark 12:29).*

*"...there is **one God**; and there is none other but he"* *(Mark 12:32).*

*"...none is good, save **one**, that is, **God**"* *(Luke 18:19).*

*"...we have **one** Father, even **God**"* *(John 8:41).*

*"I honor my Father...there is **one** that seeketh and judgeth"* [Jesus speaking] *(John 8:49-50).*

*"Seeing it is **one God** which shall justify..."* *(Romans 3:30).*

*"...there is none other **God** but **one**"* *(I Corinthians 8:4).*

*"But to us there is but **one** God, the Father"* *(I Corinthians 8:6).*

*"Now a mediator is not a mediator of one, but **God** is **one**"* *(Galatians 3:20).*

*"**One God** and Father of all, who is above all"* *(Ephesians 4:6).*

159

"For there is one God, and one mediator between God and men, the man Christ Jesus" (I Timothy 2:5).

"Thou believest that there is one God; thou doest well" (James 2:19).

"Draw nigh to God...there is one lawgiver, who is able to save and to destroy" (James 4:8, 12).

"But ye have an unction from the Holy One" (I John 2:20).

"...behold, a throne was set in heaven, and one sat on the throne" [*"Lord God Almighty" v. 8*] *(Revelation 4:2).*

Who is Jesus Christ?

The Scriptures teach that Jesus is the supernaturally conceived, virgin-born, sinless, human Son of God; Savior, redeemer, Messiah, fore-ordained ruler of this planet for the coming 1000 years, and the only way to God, **who never claimed to be "God."** In fact, Jesus denied being God *(Matt. 19:17)*; he denied making himself equal with God with these words, *"I said I am the Son of God" (John 10:36)*; and he said plainly that the Father is *"the only true God" (John 17:3)*. He said, *"my Father is greater than I" (John 14:28)*, only the Father knows the day and hour of my return *(Mark 13:32)*, and my Father will decide who sits on my right hand and on my left in **my own kingdom**, that *"is not mine to* *give" (Matt. 20:23).* Jesus claimed the Father as his God just as the Father is our God *(Matt. 27:46; John 20:17; Rev. 3:12).* He claimed that he himself is the *"Christ,"* the Anointed One, the *"Messiah" (Matt. 16:16-17; Luke 4:18; Acts 4:27; John 4:25-26).* The apostle Paul agreed. He said *"there is but one God, the Father" (I Cor. 8:6),* there is *"One God and Father of all, who is above all" (Eph. 4:6),* *"the only wise God"* is *"invisible" (I Tim. 1:17)* and *"the head of Christ is God,"* just as *"the head of every man is Christ" (I Cor. 11:3).* He said that God our Father is also the God of Jesus Christ *(II Cor. 11:31; Eph. 1:3, 17).* Paul's first sermon after his encounter with Jesus on the Damascus road was *"that he is the Son of God"* [not God]. He desired *"That ye may with one mind and one mouth glorify **God, even the Father** of our Lord Jesus Christ" (Rom. 15:6),* and he encouraged Christians *"to serve **the living and true God**; and to wait for **his Son** from heaven" (I Thess. 1:9-10).*

What about Elohim?

The Hebrew noun for God is *Elohim,* and because it can have plural connotations, some see in it a *plurality of persons* in the Deity. In light of the whole of Scripture, including the sixty-five verses cited, this is doctrinal nonsense. Elohim is used of the one true God some 2300 times in the Bible and every last time it takes a **singular** verb! Concerning Genesis 1:1, *"In the beginning God* [Elohim] *created the heavens and the earth,"* the Trinitarian scholars who translated the NIV Study Bible are forced by the facts to say in their *text-notes*:

*"God created. The Hebrew noun Elohim, is plural **but the verb is singular**, a normal usage in the O.T. when reference is to the one*

*true God. This use of the plural expresses intensification **rather than number** and has been called the **plural of majesty**, or of **potentiality**"* [emphasis mine].

The noted Trinitarian scholar Professor Charles C. Ryrie says regarding the noun Elohim: *"To conclude plurality of persons from the name itself is dubious" (Basic Theology; p. 58).* Of course some people will grasp at any straw in an effort to support their mistaken tradition.

The influence of a pagan named Plato
There is not one verse of Scripture that says that God is "three" of anything! Not "three co-equal, co-eternal persons," "one God in three persons," "three persons of one essence" or "three manifestations of one God." The terms "Trinity," "Triune," "Blessed Trinity," "Holy Trinity," "God the Son," "God the Holy Spirit," "God incarnate," "God in flesh," "two natures," and "the Deity of Christ" are not biblical terminology. Their use is a sure ticket to a misunderstanding of who God is, and the serious error of robbing our heavenly Father of His glory as the one and only Most High God!

So how did Christianity fall into this mistaken view of God? The shocking answer to that question is, we followed a blind guide, the pagan philosopher Plato. It is an indisputable fact of history that Plato was teaching a doctrine of the Trinity in his Academy in Athens, Greece, 375 years **before** the birth of Jesus Messiah. The ancient Greeks even had a city named Hagia Triada (Holy Trinity). According to the noted 20th century historian Will Durant, Plato had a weird fascination with triangles and the numeral *three*. Look at the "threes" that fascinated him. He saw **three** elements in nature, *fire, wind and water*. He saw **three** things at work in nature, *motion, creation* and a *soul* or principle of life. The soul or principle of life has **three** parts, *desire, will* and *thought*. Each part has its own *virtue* **(three)**, *moderation, courage* and *wisdom*. Beauty lies in **three**, *fitness, symmetry* and *order*. A work of art should have **three** features, *head, trunk* and *limbs*. Love is the pursuit of beauty, and has **three** stages, love of the *body*, the *soul* or of *truth*. The soul of a man has **three** parts, *mind, aspirations* and *sensations*. An ideal society has **three** parts, *productive* (workers), *protective* (warriors), and *governing* (rulers). But his "**three**" that has permeated Christian doctrine and still troubles the understanding of millions of Christians today is, his triune view of God! It consists of: 1. The Good, or first cause - "**God**." 2. The changeless Ideas, Reason, Wisdom or Mind of God - the "**Logos**." 3. A soul or principle - the "**Spirit**" of all things. *(The Life of Greece; p. 510-518).*

Trinitarian professors Roger Olson and Christopher Hall make the following shocking statement in their book, *The Trinity*:

> *"Very early in the history of theology, reflection began to focus on the **immanent Trinity** as church fathers became obsessed with **Greek ideas...**" (p. 110).*

Trinitarian scholar Millard Erickson says in his work, *God In Three Persons*:

> *"We have observed that the specific meta-physical vehicle used to express **the classical doctrine of the Trinity** as originally formulated was a **Greek metaphysics**... . While it is customary to assume that the major philosophical influence on the Greek [church] fathers was **Plato** and the **Stoics**, Durant believes the influence of **Aristotle** should not be overlooked" (p. 211, 259).* (What do Plato and Aristotle have to do with Christian doctrine?

Erickson says regarding the great 19th century religious historian Adolf Harnack:

> *"He finds the Christian community **borrowing heavily from Greek philosophy. It is from these foreign sources, not from Jesus himself, that the doctrine of the Trinity, the incarnation,** and related conceptions grew" (God In Three Persons; p. 102).*

Trinitarian professor Shirley C. Guthrie, Jr. writes in his book *Christian Doctrine*:

> *"**The Bible does not teach the doctrine of the Trinity.** The language of the doctrine is the language of the ancient church **taken from classical Greek philosophy**" (p. 76-77).*

The very educated apostle Paul knew how insidious this Greek philosophy is and warned against it strongly in Colossians 2:8:

> *"**Beware** lest any man spoil you through* *philosophy and vain deceit, after the **tradition of*** *men, after the rudiments of the world, and not* *after Christ."* Note: Philosophy is *"Greek"* philosophy, Greek in origin, and Plato is its father. As Ralph Waldo Emerson said, *"Plato is philosophy, and philosophy, Plato."*

Listen to Paul. *"Beware lest any man spoil you through philosophy"* - Plato!

Paul knew that after his departure the church would be devastated by false teaching, so he gave the following serious warning to the elders of the church at Ephesus (and us):

> *"For I know this, that after my departing shall* *grievous **wolves** enter in among you, not sparing* *the flock. Also **of your own selves** shall men* *arise, speaking perverse things, to draw away* *disciples after them. Therefore watch, and* *remember, that by the space of three years I* *ceased not to warn every one night and day **with*** *tears" (Acts 20:29-31).*

And regrettably it did happen! After the death of Paul and the other Apostles, men began to be *"converted"* who history plainly says were followers of Plato and who became *"Christian philosophers."* The list includes Justin Martyr (110-165 A.D.), Clement of Alexandria (150-215 A.D.), Origen (185-254 A.D.), Athanasius (297-373 A.D.) and Augustine (354-430 A.D.). They

165

brought with them their Platonic concept of a triune God and *"began to sprinkle nuggets of Trinitarian ore"* in their writings *"that will later be mined and purified"* (Olson and Hall; The Trinity; p. 17).

The Encyclopedia Britannica says of this Platonic influence:

> *"From the middle of the 2nd century A.D.,* ***Christians*** *who had some training in* ***Greek philosophy*** *began to feel the need to express their faith in* ***its terms...*** *The philosophy that suited them best was* ***Platonism.*** *The first Christian to use* ***Greek philosophy*** *in the service of the Christian faith was Justin Martyr. Each of the great* ***Christian Platonists*** *understood Platonism and applied it to the understanding of his faith in his own individual way. But the* ***Christian Platonism*** *that had the widest, deepest, and most lasting influence in the West was that of St. Augustine of Hippo. In his theology, insofar as Augustine's thought about God was* ***Platonic***, *he conformed fairly closely to the general pattern of Christian Platonism... .* ***Perhaps the most distinctive influence of Plotinian Neo-Platonism on Augustine's thinking about God*** *was in his* ***Trinitarian theology.*** *Because he thought that something like the* ***Christian doctrine of the Trinity*** *was to be found in Plotinus and Porphyry* [two pagan thinkers - followers of Plato], *he tended to*

166

> *regard it as a **philosophical doctrine** and tried to make philosophical sense of it... ." (Britannica - Macropaedia; Vol. 25; p. 903-904).*

A God consisting of two persons

In 325 A.D. the Roman emperor Constantine convened the Council of Nicea to settle a very heated dispute between the bishops of two cities, Alexandria and Antioch, regarding the relationship between Jesus Christ and God the Father. This dispute was troubling his empire and he desperately needed to resolve it.

After thirty days of debate, Constantine arose from the gold chair on which he had presided over the meetings and gave a lengthy speech, just before the issue was decided by majority vote. The speech was recorded by Eusebius, *"the father of church history"* who was present, and takes up twenty pages of a large history book in my library. Shockingly, in this gathering that was about to decide for Christianity for the next 1700 years the all important question, *"Who is Jesus Christ?,"* the emperor did not quote one Bible verse; not one word from Peter, Paul, John, James, Jude or Jesus himself. Who did he quote? Plato! Yes, the homosexual, pagan, Greek philosopher, Plato! He called Plato *"the gentlest and most refined of all"* and credited him with teaching us the doctrine of the *"**second God**...distinguishing them numerically as **two**...and the being of the **second Deity** proceeding from the first."* He says, *"Plato's sentiments were sound"* and *"a doctrine not merely to be admired, but profitable too."* He went on to quote the demon inspired priestess who spoke as an oracle at the temple of Apollo at

Erythrea, the demon oracle at Cuma, and the Romans Cicero and Virgil. *(The Nicene and Post-Nicene Fathers; Vol. 1; p. 566-576).* It was in this atmosphere that the 300 bishops voted that Jesus is God just as the Father is God, *"of one substance with the Father."* Thus Christianity arrived at a doctrine of God consisting of **two persons**, Father God the Creator, and Jesus the *"Divine Logos."* (Remember, the second member of **Plato's Trinity** was the *Logos*).

The birth of the Christian doctrine of the Trinity

As late as the year 350 A.D. there was still no Christian doctrine of the Trinity on this planet! However, fifty-six years after Nicea, in 381 A.D., the emperor Theodosius called the Council of Constantinople to try and settle the continuing quarrel regarding the personhood of God. Three bishops from the province of Cappadocia in Asia Minor, also followers of Plato, had supposedly figured it out; *there is one God who exists as **three Persons**.* They came to be called *"the three Cappadocians"* and one, Gregory of Nazianzus, presided over the Council. After much bitter wrangling the views of the three Cappadocians won out, and this council of 186 bishops adopted the *"Creed of Constantinople."* It states in part:

> *"We believe in the **Holy Spirit**, the Lord, the giver of life, who proceeds from the Father and the Son. With the Father and the Son **he is worshiped and glorified"*** *(Encyclopedia Americana; Vol. 20; p. 310).* Note: According to Jesus, Peter, and Paul the Holy Spirit is not a third person of God, but rather the Spirit of the

168

Father *(Matt. 10:20; Mark 13:11; John 15:26; Luke 4:18; Luke 24:49; Isa. 61:1; Acts 2:17, 33; Rom. 8:11; Eph. 3:14-16).* (The third member of **Plato's Trinity** was the *"soul - principle - Spirit - of all things".*).

Thus for the first time in history, Christianity had a doctrine of *"three persons in one God,"* the Trinity. The doctrine of Plato had prevailed! Consider the following quotes:

Trinitarian scholar Charles C. Ryrie:

> *"**In the second half of the fourth century**, three theologians from the province of Cappadocia in eastern Asia Minor **gave definitive shape to the doctrine of the Trinity...**" (Basic Theology; p. 65).*

Trinitarian Baptist professor Millard J. Erickson:

> *"What Athanasius did was to extend his teaching **about the Word** to the Spirit, **so that God exists eternally as a Triad** sharing one identical and indivisible substance. The **Cappadocians** - Basil, Gregory of Nazianzus, and Gregory of Nyssa - **developed the doctrine of the Spirit, and thus of the Trinity, further**" (God In Three Persons; p. 90).*

Harper-Collins Encyclopedia of Catholicism:

> *"**Trinitarian doctrine as such emerged in the fourth century**, due largely to the efforts of **Athanasius** and the **Cappadocians...** . The doctrine of the Trinity **formulated in the late fourth century** thus affirms that the **one God** exists as **three Persons**" (p. 1271).*

Collier's Encyclopedia:

> *"Of the many who wrote on theology...**Basil** of Caesarea (fourth century), who, with his brother, **Gregory** of Nyssa, and their friend, **Gregory** of Nazianzus, **fixed the orthodox formulation of the doctrine of the Trinity**" (Vol. 9; p. 41-42).*

Encyclopedia Britannica:

> *"**The Greek philosophical theology that developed during the Trinitarian controversies** over the relationships among **the persons of the Godhead**, which were **settled at the ecumenical councils of Nicea (325) and Constantinople (381)**, owed a great deal to Origen on both sides, orthodox and heretical. Its most important representatives on the orthodox side were the **three Christian Platonist** [i.e. followers of Plato] theologians of Cappadocia, **Basil** of Caesarea, **Gregory** of Nazianzus, and Basil's brother **Gregory** of Nyssa*" (Macropaedia; Vol. 25; p. 903).*

Nineteenth century historian Adolph Harnack:

> *"The* **Cappadocians** *were still relatively independent theologians,* **worthy disciples and admirers of Origen**, *using* **new forms** *to make* **the faith of Athanasius** *intelligible to contemporary thought, and thus* **establishing them**, *though with modifications"* (*History of Dogma; Vol. 3; p. 151*). *"***Gregory** *(of Nyssa) was able to demonstrate the application of the* **incarnation** *more definitely than Athanasius could... . But he does so by the aid of* **a thoroughly Platonic idea** *which is only slightly suggested in Athanasius,* **and is not really covered by Biblical reference**" (*History of Dogma; Vol. 3; p. 297*).

Collier's Encyclopedia:

> *"During the* **4th century**...**the content of Christian dogma was developed**...*by the very able men who have come to be known as the* **Fathers of the Church**. *Living in the eastern part of the Roman Empire, and writing in* **Greek**, *were* **St. Basil** *of Caesarea,* **St. Gregory** *of Nyssa, and* **St. Gregory** *of Nazianzus.* **These men continued the speculative and Platonist tendencies of Clement and Origen**..." (*Vol. 15; p. 318*).

The Encyclopedia Britannica sums it up well:

> *"Although Athanasius prepared the ground, constructive **agreement on the central doctrine of the Trinity was not reached in his lifetime (297-373 A.D.). The decisive contribution to the Trinitarian argument** was made by a remarkable group of philosophically minded theologians from Cappadocia - **Basil** of Caesarea, his younger brother **Gregory** of Nyssa, and his lifelong friend **Gregory** of Nazianzus. So far as **Trinitarian dogma** is concerned, **the Cappadocians succeeded...in formulating a conception of God as three Persons in one essence** that eventually proved generally acceptable"* (Macropaedia; Vol. 16; p. 319). Note: Athanasius died in **373 A.D.**, but *"agreement on the central doctrine of the Trinity was not reached in his lifetime."* What? **Athanasius died in 373 A.D., but *"agreement on the central doctrine of the Trinity was not reached in his lifetime."* WOW!**

The above statement is shocking since the great majority of Christians today believe in the non-biblical doctrine of the Trinity. Again regarding the Cappadocians: *"So far as **Trinitarian dogma** is concerned, the **Cappadocians** succeeded...in formulating a conception of **God as three Persons in one essence** that eventually proved generally **acceptable"** (at Constantinople in **381 A.D.**).*

Emperor Theodosius, who convened the Council of Constantinople, issued the following edict to enforce this Trinitarian doctrine:

> *"It is Our will that all peoples ruled by the administration of Our Clemency shall practice that religion which the divine Peter the Apostle transmitted to the Romans...**we shall believe in** the single deity of the Father, the Son, and the Holy Ghost under the concept of **equal majesty** and of **the Holy Trinity**. We **command** that persons who follow this rule shall embrace the name of catholic Christians. **The rest**, however, **whom We judge demented and insane**, shall carry the infamy of heretical dogmas. Their meeting places shall not receive the name of churches, and **they shall be smitten** first by Divine Vengeance, and secondly by **the retribution of hostility which We shall assume** in accordance with the Divine Judgement"* (A.D. 381 Heretics, Pagans, and the Dawn of the Monotheistic State; Charles Freeman; p. 25).

And sure enough, since that time anyone who has dared oppose this **Platonic error** has found his *person* or his *character* under attack by its most zealous adherents!

My friend, you will be judged by God for what you do with your knowledge of the above facts!

Proof that I John 5:7 is a later insertion, a forgery

- Author Lee Strobel in his book, *The Case For Christ*, interviewed the late Bruce M. Metzger, PH.D., who was at that time an 84 year old authority on the authenticity of the N.T., who had authored or edited fifty books relating to the subject. He put the *"grand total of (early) Greek manuscripts at 5,664."* Metzger tells Strobel that if someone challenges the authenticity of I John 5:7: *"For there are three that bear record in heaven, the Father, the Word, and the Holy Ghost: and these three are one,"* saying *"that's not in the earliest manuscripts,"* his answer would be, ***"and that's true enough.*** *I think that these words are found in only about seven or eight copies (manuscripts), all from the fifteenth or sixteenth century.* ***I acknowledge that is not what the author of I John was inspired to write."*** Strobel and Metzger, both **trinitarian** in belief, were casting doubt on one of the main scriptures Trinitarians use to support their doctrine.

- The NIV quotes in its *text **notes*** the words *"the Father, the Word and the Holy Spirit, and these three are one. And there are three that testify on earth,"* and then explains **why they are not included in the text** of the NIV. They say, ***"the addition is not found in any Greek manuscript or N.T. translation prior to the 16th century."*** These words are also not found in the *New Revised Standard Version,* the *New American Standard Bible,* the *English Standard Version,* the *Holman Christian Standard Bible* or the *New Living Translation.*

- Respected **trinitarian** Biblical scholar Professor Charles C. Ryrie agrees. Writing in his well known work, *Basic Theology,* he states:

  > *"The N.T. contains no explicit statement of the doctrine of the triunity of God (since 'these three are one' in I John 5:7 **is apparently not a part of the genuine text of Scripture)**" (p. 60).* *"**It is fair to say that the Bible does not clearly teach the doctrine of the Trinity. In fact, there is not even one proof text**..." (p. 89).*

- **Trinitarian** Millard J. Erickson (Southern Baptist) in his book, *God In Three Persons,* says that some oppose the doctrine of the Trinity because of:

  > *"....the **apparent silence** of the Bible on this important subject. This contention notes that **there really is no explicit statement of the doctrine of the Trinity in the Bible**, particularly since the revelation by textual criticism of the **spurious nature** of I John 5:7. Other passages have been seen on closer study to be applicable **only under the greatest of strain**. It is unlikely that any text of Scripture can be shown to teach **the doctrine of the Trinity** in a clear, direct, and unmistakable fashion" (p. 108-109).*

- The Wycliffe Bible Commentary says of I John 5:7:

    "The text of this verse should read, 'Because there are three that bear record.' **The remainder of the verse is spurious.** *Not a single manuscript contains the* **trinitarian addition** *before the fourteenth century, and the verse is never quoted in the controversies over the Trinity in the first 450 years of the Church era."*

- The New Bible Commentary says regarding I John 5:7:

    "The whole of verse 7 of the Authorized Version is omitted in the Revised Version because **it was not written by John.**"

One question in closing. Who would have had the audacity to commit such an act of forgery? I say this with compassion for a fellow human being, but he might be in hell today for inserting his uninspired words into God's Holy Bible (see *Rev. 22:18-19*). Please do not follow his error!

Conclusion: We must trust Jesus that **he** is a supernaturally conceived, virgin-born, unique **human being**, the sinless Son of God. Also, we as Christians must come into agreement with our Lord Jesus Messiah regarding these awesome truths **about God.** Only then will we be *"unto God a sweet aroma of Christ"* (2 Cor. *2:15)*, and remove the smell of Plato from our garments! (See my book *Glory To God In The Highest*--Removing The Influence of Socrates, Plato, Philo and Greek Philosophy From Christian Doctrine. Note: The busts and paintings of Socrates (a pedophile)

176

and Plato (a homosexual) have places of honor in the Vatican, because the Catholic church acknowledges their notable contributions to Christian doctrine!).   Only then will we "increase in favor with God" as Jesus did *(Luke 2:52)*, that we might have signs, healings, miracles, and Apostolic power for the end time , as God has promised us *(Daniel 11:32; John 14:12)*.

Jesus or Plato?

It is a fact of history that Plato was teaching a doctrine of the Trinity in his academy in Athens, 375 years before the birth of Jesus.

Emperor Constantine (325 A.D.)..."Plato himself declared, with truth, a God exalted above every essence, but to him he added also a second, distinguishing them as two...the second Deity proceeding from the first" (addressing the Nicean Council, before they voted that Jesus is God, just as the Father is God).

Thomas Jefferson..."I fear that believers will follow Platonizing Christians...that they will give up Jesus for Plato."

Encyclopedia Britannica..."Each of the great Christian Platonists ["Justin Martyr - Clement - Origen - St. Augustine"] understood Platonism and applied it to the understanding of his faith... ."

Trinitarian scholar Millard Erickson..."We have observed that the metaphysical vehicle used to express the classical doctrine of the Trinity as originally formulated was a Greek metaphysics... . While it is customary to assume that the major philosophical influence on the Greek fathers was Plato and the Stoics, Durrant believes the influence of Aristotle should not be overlooked."

Trinitarian scholars R. Olson and C. Hall..."Very early in the history of theology, reflection began to focus more and more on the imminent Trinity as church fathers became obsessed with Greek ideas... ."

Trinitarian professor Shirley C. Guthrie, Jr...."The Bible does not teach the doctrine of the Trinity. The language of the doctrine is the language of the ancient church taken from classical Greek philosophy."

Chapter 28

God Declaring Himself

$\mathcal{N}$ o one is qualified to define who God is but God Himself, or those in whom He has placed His own words, i.e. His Son Jesus Messiah and his chosen Apostles.

> *"For he whom God hath sent speaketh the **words** of God"* [Jesus speaking] *(John 3:34).*

> *"For I have given unto them the **words** which thou gavest me"* [Jesus' prayer to the Father] *(John 17:8).*

Jesus spoke the very words of God, but there is nothing more powerful in Scripture than the **Lord God** Almighty, our heavenly **Father** Himself, declaring who He is!

Exodus 3:15:

> *"And God said moreover unto Moses, Thus shalt thou say unto the children of Israel, **the Lord God** of your fathers, the God of Abraham, the God of Isaac, and the God of Jacob, hath sent me unto you: **this is my name for ever**, and this is my memorial unto **all generations**."*

Exodus 34:5-6:

*"And the Lord descended in the cloud, and stood with him there, and **proclaimed the name of the Lord**. And the Lord passed by before him, and proclaimed, The Lord, The **Lord God**, merciful and gracious, longsuffering, and abundant in goodness and truth..."*

Isaiah 37:23: [God says]

*"Whom hast thou reproached and blasphemed? And against whom hast thou exalted thy voice, and lifted up thine eyes on high? Even against the **Holy One** of Israel."*

Isaiah 40:25:

*"To **whom** then will ye liken me or shall I be **equal**? saith the Holy **One**."* Note: God our Father is the Holy **One** with **no equal**! This verse destroys the doctrine of the Trinity, that teaches **three** persons who are **co-equal**.

Isaiah 43:10-11:

*"Ye are my witnesses, saith the Lord, and my servant whom I have chosen: that ye may know and believe me, and understand that I am he: **before me there was no God formed, neither shall there be after me**. I, even I, am the Lord; **and beside me there is no saviour**."* Note: God is our ultimate *"savior,"* but He has used *"saviors"* *(Neh. 9:27; Obad. v.21; Luke 1:47; Acts 5:31; Acts 13:23; I Tim. 4:10; Jude v. 25).*

Isaiah 44:6:

*"Thus saith the Lord the King of Israel, and his redeemer the Lord of hosts; I am the first, and **I** am the last; and **beside me there is no God**."* Notice carefully the personal pronoun *"I."* **One** *entity, being, person* is speaking - not three!

Isaiah 44:8:

*"Fear ye not, neither be afraid: have not I told thee from that time, and have declared it? Ye are even my witnesses. **Is there a God beside me?** Yea, **there is no God; I know not any**."*

Isaiah 44:24:

*"Thus saith the Lord, thy redeemer, and he that formed thee from the womb, **I am the Lord** that maketh all things; **that stretcheth forth the heavens alone; that spreadeth abroad the earth by myself**."*

Isaiah 45:5-6:

*"**I am the Lord, and there is none else, there is no God beside me**: That they may know from the rising of the sun, and from the west, that there is **none beside me. I am the Lord, and there is none else**."*

Isaiah 45:11-12:

*"Thus saith the Lord, **the Holy One of Israel, and his Maker. I have made the earth**, and created man upon*

181

*it: I, even **my hands, have stretched out the heavens,** and all their host have I commanded."*

Isaiah 45:18:

"For thus saith the Lord that created the heavens; God himself that formed the earth and made it; *he hath established it, he created it not in vain, he formed it to be inhabited:* ***I am the Lord; and there is none else."***

Isaiah 45:21-22:

*"Tell ye, and bring them near; yea, let them take counsel together: who hath declared this from ancient time? Who hath told it from that time? Have not I the Lord? and **there is no God else beside me**; a just God and a Saviour; **there is none beside me.** Look unto me, and be ye saved, all the ends of the earth: for **I am God, and there is none else."***

Isaiah 46:9:

*"Remember the former things of old: **for I am God, and there is none else;** I am God, and there is **none like me."***

Hosea 13:4:

*"Yet I am the Lord thy God from the land of Egypt, **and thou shalt know no god but me: for there is no saviour besides me."***

<u>Joel 2:27:</u>

> *"And ye shall know that I am in the midst of Israel, and that **I am the Lord your God, and none else**."*

Could anything be clearer? Could God have said it any plainer? Let me ask you a question. What part of "one," "alone," "none else," "by myself," or "none beside me," don't we understand? "**I am God the Creator, I am one, I am alone**." My friend, hasten to come into agreement with **God** regarding this most important truth!

The Holy One With No Equal

"Say unto the cities of Judah, Behold your God!

Behold, the Lord God will come with strong hand"

(Isaiah 40:9-10).

"To whom then will ye liken me, or shall I be equal?

saith the Holy One" (Isaiah 40:25).

Chapter 29

Is Jesus Equal With God?

"My Father, which gave them me, is greater than all" [Jesus speaking] (John 10:29).

"... my Father is greater than I" [Jesus speaking] (John 14:28).

"But I would have you know, that...the head of Christ is God" (1 Cor. 11:3).

"...the kingdom of our God, and the power of his Christ" (Revelation 12:10).

If we embrace the doctrine taught by most of Christianity, that Jesus was equal with God the Father before his birth, then we are forced to conclude that God tricked him. Because after Jesus' sinless life and sacrificial death, he was exalted to *"the right hand of the throne of God"* (Heb. 12:2), a position subservient to the Father! In fact God calls him *"my servant"* (Isa. 42:1; 53:11). In the Apostles' prayer to God the Creator in Acts chapter four, they referred to Jesus twice as "thy holy child Jesus" (vs. 27,30). The word "child" in these verses is the Greek word "pais", (Strong's #3816), and it means "servant boy." So to these early Christians, Jesus was God the Father's **servant boy**. Check it out! And Paul says that after Jesus' 1000-year reign on earth the Son will forever

185

be *"**subject**"* (Gk. *hupotasso - Strongs #5293 - "**beneath -
subordinate - put under - in an inferior position**"*) to the Father *(I
Cor. 15:24-28).*

Of course Jesus never once reached for equality with the Father, or
claimed that position for himself.   Several years after he had
ascended to heaven, Jesus made this awesome statement:

> *"To him that overcometh will I grant to sit with
> me in **my throne**, even as I also overcame, and
> am set down with **my Father** in **his throne**"
> (Rev. 3:21).*   Note: According to Jesus, the
> throne in heaven is the **Father's** throne. See also
> Luke 1:32.

This agrees with twelve other N.T. scriptures.

> *"So then, after the Lord had spoken unto them,
> he was received up into heaven, and sat down on
> the right hand of God" (Mark 16:19).*

> *"Therefore being by the right hand of God
> exalted, and having received **of the Father** the
> promise of the Holy Ghost" (Acts 2:33).*

> *"But he* [Stephen] *looked up into heaven, and
> saw the glory of **God**, and Jesus standing on the
> right hand of God" (Acts 7:55).*

*"Behold, I see the heavens opened, and the Son of Man standing on the **right hand** of God" (Acts 7:56).*

*"It is Christ that died...who is even at the **right hand** of God" (Rom. 8:34).*

"Which he [God the Father] *wrought in Christ...and set him at his own **right hand** in the heavenly places" (Eph. 1:20).*

*"...seek those things which are above, where Christ sitteth on the **right hand** of God" (Col. 3:1).*

[The Son] *"sat down on the **right hand** of the Majesty on high" (Heb. 1:3).*

*"We have such a **high priest**, who is set on the **right hand** of the throne of the Majesty in the heaven" (Heb. 8:1).*

*"But **this man**, after he had offered one sacrifice for sins for ever, sat down on the **right hand** of God" (Heb. 10:12).*

"Looking unto Jesus [who] *...is set down at the **right hand** of the throne of God" (Heb. 12:2).*

> *"Who is gone into heaven, and is on the right*
> *hand of God" (I Peter 3:22).*

Question. Why should we be surprised that Jesus is now seated at the **right hand** of God in heaven? This is exactly what God promised him according to Psalm 110:1:

> *"The Lord said unto my Lord, sit thou at my*
> *right hand, until I make thine enemies thy*
> *footstool."* Note: Peter teaches in Acts 2:30-35
> that Psalm 110:1 is God the Father speaking to
> Jesus Messiah.

To my Christian family: **Stop giving Jesus, God's throne in heaven, and making him co-equal with the Father! That is blindness bordering on idolatry!**

Chapter 30

Jesus Is Our Brother

"For whom he [God] *did foreknow, he also did predestinate to be conformed to the image of his Son, that he might be the **firstborn** among **many brethren"** (Rom. 8:29).*

*"And call no man your father upon the earth: for one is your **Father**, which is in heaven. Neither be ye called masters: for one is your **Master**, even Christ" (Matt. 23:9-10).*

*J*esus never claimed to be our *"heavenly Father,"* he is our brother. The following chapter is written to prove from Scripture that very important truth.

*"I will raise them up a Prophet **from among their brethren**, like unto thee..."* [God to Moses] *(Deut. 18:18).*

[Philip to **Nathanael concerning Jesus]** *"We have **found him**, of whom **Moses** in the law, and the prophets did write..." (John 1:45).*

[Peter regarding Jesus] *"For Moses truly said unto the fathers, a Prophet shall the Lord your God raise up unto you **of your brethren**, like unto me..."(Acts 3:22).*

[Stephen preaching Jesus] *"This is that Moses, which said...a **Prophet** shall the Lord your God raise up unto you **of your brethren**..." (Acts 7:37).*

[Jesus] *"For whosoever shall do the will of **my Father which is in heaven**, the same is **my brother**, and sister, and mother" (Matt. 12:50).*

[Jesus] *"And the King shall answer and say unto them, Verily I say unto you, Inasmuch as ye have done it unto one of the least of these **my brethren**, ye have done it unto me" (Matt. 25:40).*

[Jesus] *"...**my brethren** are these which hear the word of God, and do it" (Luke 8:21).*

[Jesus to Mary at the tomb] *"...but go to **my brethren**, and say unto them, I ascend unto my Father, and your Father; and to my God, and your God" (John 20:17).*

*"For **both** he that sanctifieth and they who are sanctified **are all of one**: for which cause he* [Jesus] *is not ashamed to call them **brethren**, Saying, I will declare thy name **unto my brethren**, in the midst of the church will I* [Jesus] *sing praise unto thee* [God]*" (Heb. 2:11-12).*

> *"Wherefore in **all things** it behooved him to be made like unto **his brethren**...to make reconciliation for the sins of the people" (Heb. 2:17).*

Joint-heirs with Christ

The apostle Paul has much to say in Romans chapter eight regarding Christians being *"children"* or *"sons"* of God.

> *"For as many as are led by the Spirit of God, they are the sons of God. ...ye have received the Spirit of adoption, whereby **we cry**, Abba Father. ...we are the children of God: And if children, then heirs; **heirs of God**, and **joint-heirs with Christ**; if so that we suffer **with him**, that we may be **also glorified together**" (Rom. 8:14-17).*

The word Paul uses for *"joint-heirs"* is *"sugkleronomos"* in the Greek *(Strongs #4789)*, and it means *"a co-heir, i.e. participant in common: - fellow heir, heir together, heir with."* This is the same word Paul uses in Ephesians 3:6 when he speaks of the *"mystery"* that was previously hidden:

> *"That the Gentiles should be **fellow heirs** [with Israel], and of the same body, and partakers of his [God's] promise in Christ by the Gospel" (Eph. 3:6).*

This is the same Greek word (*sugkleronomos*) that Peter uses in I Peter 3:7 when he says that husbands and wives should live together peaceably, *"as being **heirs together** of the grace of life."*

Please accept the fact that the only way we as Christians can be **co-heirs - fellow heirs - heirs in common,** with Christ, is if he [Jesus] is our brother.   Of course, as our elder brother [*"the firstborn among many brethren"* Rom. 8:29], under God's rules of inheritance, Jesus receives the **double portion** of glory, rulership, etc.   In fact our sonship is based solely on our being **in** Christ Jesus and partakers of his Sonship.   Listen to Paul again:

> *"And because ye are sons, God hath sent forth*
> *the Spirit of his Son into your hearts, crying,*
> *Abba Father.   **Wherefore** thou art no more a*
> *servant, but **a son**; and if a son, then **an heir of***
> ***God through Christ"** (Gal. 4:6-7).*

A very important key to understanding this is what the apostle John writes concerning Jesus' glory.   Notice closely his words in John 1:14:

> *"And we beheld **his glory**, the glory **as of the***
> ***only begotten of the Father....** "*

This is Jesus' glory!   Now study closely Jesus' words to the Father [as recorded by John] in John 17:21-23:

> *"That they all may be one; as thou Father, art in*
> *me, and I in thee, that **they also may be one in***
> ***us....** .   And **the glory which thou gavest me I***
> ***have given them**: that they may be one, even as*

192

*we are one: **I in them, and thou in me**, that they may know **that thou hast loved them**, as thou hast loved me."* Wow! What is that again precious Jesus? *"**Father...thou hast loved them, as thou hast loved me."***

John sheds more light regarding **our sonship** in I John 3:1-3:

*"Behold, what manner of love **the Father** hath bestowed upon us, that **we** should be called **the sons of God**... . Beloved, now are **we the sons of God**, and it doth not yet appear what we shall be: but we know that, **when he shall appear** [our Father, God], we shall be like him; for **we shall see him** as he is. And every man that hath this hope in him purifieth himself, **even as he is pure"** (I John 3:1-3).* Compare this with Jesus' words in Matthew 5:8, *"Blessed are the **pure in heart**, for they shall **see God."*** (See also *Rev. 1:4; 1:8; 4:8; 11:17; 16:5;* *"...**which is to come"***).

Understanding the law of redemption

The following verses teach us that Jesus Christ has redeemed us by his sinless life, his sacrificial death, and his shed blood.

*"Christ hath **redeemed** us from the curse of the law, being made a curse for us" (Gal. 3:13).*

*"God sent forth his Son...To **redeem** them that were under the law, that we might receive the adoption of sons" (Gal. 4:4-5).*

*" [Jesus Christ] In whom we have **redemption** through his blood, the forgiveness of sins" (Eph. 1:7).*

*"...our Savior Jesus Christ; Who gave himself for us, that he might **redeem** us from all iniquity" (Titus 2:13-14).*

*"...by his own blood he entered in once into the holy place, having obtained eternal **redemption** for us" (Heb. 9:12).*

*"...ye were not **redeemed** with corruptible things, as silver or gold...But with the precious blood of Christ, as of a lamb without blemish" (I Peter 1:18-19).*

*"Thou art worthy to take the book, and to open the seals thereof: for thou wast slain, and hast **redeemed** us **to God** by thy blood out of every kindred, and tongue, and people, and nation "(Rev. 5:9).*

There are several Greek words that are translated in the verses above *"redeem," "redeemed,"* or *"redemption,"* but all carry the meaning *"to ransom, purchase, or deliver by paying a price."* That is what Jesus has done for us. However, that fact tells us much regarding who he is. In Leviticus chapter twenty-five, God established **the law of redemption** by which Israel and those who serve Him were bound. Notice verse twenty-five:

> *"If thy **brother** be waxen poor, and hath sold away some of his possessions, and if **any of his kin** come to redeem it, then shall he redeem that which **his brother** sold" (Lev. 25:25).* Note: *"his brother."*

So we see that lost possessions **could only be redeemed** by *"his kin...his **brother.**"* Now consider verses 47-49 regarding one who has sold **himself**:

> *"And if a sojourner or stranger wax rich by thee, and thy **brother** that dwelleth by him wax poor, **and sell himself** unto the stranger or sojourner...after that he is sold he may be redeemed again; **one of his brethren** may redeem him: Either his uncle, or his uncle's son, may redeem him, or **any that is nigh of kin** unto him **of his family** may redeem him..." (Lev. 25:47-49).*

This is God's law of redemption. A friend, a neighbor or a stranger **could not redeem** one who was sold into slavery for an unpaid debt! He could only be redeemed by *"**one of his brethren,**"* one that is *"**nigh of kin unto him of his family.**"* Jesus could only qualify to redeem us because he is *"the **man** Christ Jesus,"* our **brother** in the *human family*! The death of a *God* could not redeem us. An *angel* could not redeem us. Jesus is a supernaturally conceived, virgin-born, unique human being, our brother; therefore he redeemed us. That is the message of the cross! Listen to Jesus:

> *"But now ye seek to kill me, **a man** that hath told you the truth, which I have heard of God"* *(John 8:40)*. Note: The word *"man"* that Jesus used is *"anthropos"* in Greek *(Strongs #444)* and it has one meaning, *"a human being."* It is the same word Jesus used over 80 times in the NT when he called himself *"Son of **man**."* Again, an *"anthropos"* - a human over 80 times. Now, compare that with the fact that Jesus never once in Scripture referred to himself as *"God,"* or *"God the Son."*

Listen to John the Baptist:

> *"After me cometh **a man** which is preferred before me"* *(John 1:30)*.

> *"...all things that John spoke of this **man** were true"* *(John 10:41)*.

> *"Behold the Lamb of God, which taketh away the sin of the world"* *(John 1:29)*. Note: *"Behold the **Lamb**... ."* Not *"God,"* but *"the **Lamb** of God."* **The message of the Gospel is**

196

not the story of a *"dying God,"* but of the death of a sinless man, our brother, *"the Lamb of God."*

Notice again Hebrews 2:17:

*"Wherefore in **all things** it behooved him* [was necessary] ***to be made like unto his brethren**...to make reconciliation for the sins of the people."*

The Kinsman Redeemer

The Old Testament book of Ruth is a beautiful story of redemption, given to teach us a lesson regarding the redemptive work of Christ. The theme of the book is the search for a Kinsman-Redeemer to redeem the lost inheritance and marry the gentile bride. The Hebrew word for Kinsman-Redeemer is *"gaal,"* pronounced gaw-al' *(Strongs #1350)*, and it means *"to be the next of kin and as such to buy back a relative's property - (an) avenger, deliverer - (to) purchase, ransom, redeem."* When they found Boaz, a type of Christ [the one from Bethlehem who is able to redeem], Naomi told Ruth, *"The man is **near of kin** unto us, one of our **kinsmen"** (Ruth 2:20)*. This fact of kinship is stated again in chapter three, verses 2, 9, and 12, and in chapter four, verses, 1, 6, and 9; which proves its utmost importance. But Boaz tells Ruth that there is another kinsman who must be given the chance to *"do the kinsman's part: but if he will not do the part of a kinsman to thee, then I will do the part of a kinsman to thee, as the Lord liveth" (Ruth 3:13)*.

197

The other kinsman of which Boaz spoke, at first said *"I will redeem it,"* but when he saw the full picture, decided, *"I cannot redeem it"* *(Ruth 4:4, 6).* This man is a type of the *"first Adam,"* who could not save!   But Jesus Christ, *"the last Adam"* *(I Cor. 15:45),* **is mighty to save!**

> *"For since **by man** came death, **by man** came also the resurrection of the dead.   For as in Adam* [*"the first man"* *I Cor. 15:47*] *all die, even so in Christ* [*"the second Adam"* *v. 47*] *shall all be made alive"* *(I Cor. 15:21-22).*

So Jesus is our Kinsman-Redeemer, our brother who has redeemed us from the bondage of sin and death, unto God, by the sacrifice of himself on Calvary.   This understanding gives more meaning to Jesus' final words on the cross as recorded in John 19:30:   *"It is finished."*   The word *"finished"* is *"teleo"* in the Greek *(Strongs #5055)* and it means **to discharge a debt, pay in full!**

Paid in full by the blood of the **Lamb!**

Chapter 31

What About John One?

"In the beginning was the Word, and the Word was with God, and the Word was God. The same was in the beginning with God. All things were made by him; and without him was not anything made that was made. In him was life; and the life was the light of men" (v. 1-4).

*"And the Word was made flesh, and dwelt among us, (and we beheld **his glory**, the glory as of the only begotten of the Father,) full of grace and truth" (v. 14)*

*T*he above verses are at the heart of the debate as to Jesus' deity, and the key to a true biblical understanding regarding who he is. **Trinitarian** scholar Dr. Colin Brown, in his work, *Trinity and Incarnation: In Search of Contemporary Orthodoxy,* truthfully says:

> *"It is a common but patent **misreading** of the opening of John's Gospel to read it as if it said: 'In the beginning was the **Son** and the **Son** was with God and the **Son** was God.' What has happened here is **the substitution of Son for Word**, and thereby the Son is made a member of the Godhead which existed from the beginning"* (p. 88-89).

In other words, most Christian scholars believe that when John used the word *"word,"* or *"Word,"* *(Greek - **logos**)*, in the first chapter of his gospel, he had in mind a pre-existent being or second person of God, who was *"with God"* and *"was God."* The confusion arises because of the Greek philosopher Plato's use of the word *"logos"* in his teaching regarding the divine *"logos,"* a lesser being, distinct from God! Note: *"Word"* or *"word?"* The ancient Greek language had no higher or lower case so the capital *"W"* is a choice made by the editor or publisher, and does not affect the meaning of the word *"word."*

The noted **Trinitarian** scholar Professor James Dunn correctly states in his exhaustive study, *Christology In The Making:*

> *"There is no clear indication anywhere in Paul that he ever identified Christ (pre-existent or otherwise) with the **Logos** (Word) of God"* (p. 39). *"Similarly in Acts there is no sign of any christology of pre-existence"* (p. 51). *"In Matthew and Luke, Jesus' divine sonship is traced back specifically to his **birth or conception**...he was **Son of God** because his conception was **an act of creative power by the Holy Spirit**"* (p. 61). *"In the earliest period of Christianity 'Son of God' was not an obvious vehicle of a christology of incarnation or pre-existence. **Certainly such a christology cannot be traced back to Jesus himself** with any degree of conviction,...it is less likely that we can find such a christology in Paul or Mark or Luke or*

200

Matthew" (p. 64). ***"There is no indication that Jesus thought or spoke of himself as having pre-existed with God prior to his birth or appearance on earth. We cannot claim that Jesus believed himself to be the incarnate Son of God" (p. 254). Only in the Fourth Gospel*** *can we speak of a doctrine of the incarnation" (p. 259).*

Trinitarian Millard J. Erickson, wrote a book titled, *God In Three Persons.* At the time he wrote it, he was research professor of theology at Southwestern [Southern] Baptist Theological Seminary. In it he states:

> *"John is the only evangelist who identifies Jesus as divine" (p. 193).* He says again on page 210, *"He is, for example, the only Gospel writer to clearly identify the Son as divine."*

My contention is, that if Jesus, Paul, Matthew, Mark, Luke, and Peter knew nothing of a pre-existence and incarnation, **it did not happen!** John has been misunderstood! And of course, to take the word of only **one** witness would break the biblical rule for establishing truth, as set down by Moses in the Torah and endorsed by Jesus in Matthew 18:16.

> *"At the mouth of **two witnesses**, or at the mouth of **three witnesses**, shall the matter be established" (Deut. 19:15).*

As Professor Dunn says also: (Thank God for men who have the courage to say it!)

> *"There is of course always the possibility that* ***'popular pagan superstition'*** *became* ***popular*** ***Christian superstition***, *by a gradual assimilation and spread of belief"* *(p. 251).*

How did John come to be so misunderstood? For the answer to that important question we shall look briefly at history and then to the Bible.

The divine Logos doctrine

My wife LaBreeska and I currently have a ministry that is quite varied, which includes writing, singing, preaching, and teaching seminars. We minister according to the invitation, and some of it is totally evangelistic, while at other times I am invited to teach the biblical doctrine of the one Most High God, and His Son Christ Jesus. Whether or not I am called upon to teach, I always try to find time alone with the pastor or leader to share this truth one on one. We ministered in one of these evangelistic settings recently, and afterward I spoke with the very seasoned and successful pastor regarding this truth. He received the news sweetly that the Bible does not teach a Trinity or an Incarnation, but had one important question that is typical. *"But what about the Logos?"* Here is the answer to that question with statements of fact from history that cannot be refuted.

- Around 500 B.C., the famous Greek writer and thinker Heraclitus introduced to humanity the idea that the world is

governed by a *"firelike Logos,"* a **divine** force similar to **human reason**, that produces the order and pattern in nature.

- Around 430 B.C., a follower of Heraclitus, the Greek philosopher Socrates, a pedophile who is known to have been romantically involved with boys as young as 11, began his diligent search for *"logos"* in **human reason**, with intense questioning known as the "Socrates method."

- In 399 B.C., Socrates was convicted of crimes, including corrupting the youth of Athens, by a jury of 500 of his peers, and was executed in prison.

- In 386 B.C., the philosopher Plato, a homosexual Greek, the most dedicated and famous pupil of Socrates, founded a university in Athens called *"Academy."* It was dedicated to the *"worship of spirits"* and there he began to teach the doctrines of the divine logos and the triune God. Through his voluminous writings he also gave birth to *modern philosophy. (Historian Edward Gibbon; The Doctrine and Fall of The Roman Empire; Vol. 2; p. 301).*

- In 300 B.C., Zeno, the Greek philosopher, founded the first Stoic school, at Athens. The Stoics believed in the **Logos** as the *"divine reason"* and all-pervading *"breath of fire"* as handed down to them by Heraclitus, Socrates, and Plato. They strongly promoted this idea for the next several centuries. (See Acts 17:18).

- About 20 B.C., Philo Judaeus was born in Alexandria, Egypt. He was to become the most prolific writer of pre-Christian Judaism. **A follower of Plato**, he would promote his idea of the Logos (using the terms *"logos" or "divine logos"* some 1400 times in his writings) **before** Jesus began his ministry in Galilee!

After the death of the last Apostle, men began to be "converted" to Christianity who history plainly says were lovers and followers of Plato, and who became *"Christian philosophers."* They are referred to as the *"Greek church fathers"* and the list includes Justin Martyr (110-165 A.D.), Clement of Alexandria (150-215 A.D.), Origen (185-254 A.D.), Athanasius (297-373 A.D.), and Augustine (354-430 A.D.). They brought with them their **Platonic** concepts of a *divine logos* and a *triune God* from which Christianity has never recovered!

More about Philo

Much of the confusion regarding the word *"Word"* (Greek - *logos)* found in the first fourteen verses of the Gospel of John can be laid at the feet of the early first-century writer, mystic, philosopher, Philo. He was a Hellenistic Jew from the city of Alexandria, Egypt. A Hellenist was a non-Greek, especially a Jew, who as an **imitator of the Greeks**, adopted their ideas, language, customs, etc. As such, Philo the Jew was strongly influenced by the teachings of the **Greeks-Socrates, Plato,** and **Aristotle**-while at the same time, trying to hold on to his Jewish faith and its teachings of monotheism *(one God).* Because of Philo's conflicting beliefs between Judaism and Hellenism, his writings betray thinking that is often contradictory.

Since Philo was born about 20 B.C. and lived until about 50 A.D., he was already a very famous Jewish philosopher **before** the beginning of the ministries of **Jesus,** or **John, Peter, Paul** and the other N.T. writers. At the beginning of the first century, the Jewish people had not heard from God through a prophet for some 400 years, and in their backsliding were wide open to be corrupted by strange doctrines, including **Greek** and **Roman** concepts that took them away from the truth of God as set down in their Torah. Jesus and his followers dealt with this problem continually, as recorded throughout the New Testament.

> *"Teaching for doctrines the commandments of men. For laying aside the commandment of God, ye hold the tradition of men...Full well ye reject the commandment of God, that ye many keep your own tradition...Making the word of God of none effect through your tradition"* [Jesus speaking] *(Mark. 7:7-9, 13).*

> *"Hath not God made foolish the wisdom of this world? For the Jews require a sign, and **the Greeks seek after wisdom**: But we preach Christ crucified, unto the Jews a stumbling block, and unto the Greeks foolishness"* [Paul speaking] *(I Cor. 1:20-23).*

> *"**Beware** lest any man spoil you through **philosophy** and vain deceit, after the tradition of men, after the rudiments of the world, and not after Christ" (Col. 2:8).*

*"Spoil you through **philosophy!**"* It was well known even in Paul's day that Plato was the **father of philosophy**. As Ralph Waldo Emerson said, *"**Plato is philosophy, and philosophy, Plato!**"*

It is beyond question that much of pre-Christian Jewish thought had been affected by the writings of Philo, this lover and follower of Plato, including his wrong concepts regarding the Word. He was the chief proponent of the doctrine of the *"divine Logos."* This was a concept that he had borrowed from Plato and never in any way related it to Jesus of Nazareth, as he wrote well before the beginning of Jesus' ministry and never once mentioned Jesus or Christianity in his volume of work. He arrived at **his** *"divine Logos"* doctrine by mixing Judaism with the ideas of **Plato**, written some 400 years before.

For Philo the term *"logos"* seems to have had an inordinate appeal, as he used it more than 1400 times in his extensive writings. Philo often speaks of the Logos as if it were a *being* distinct from God, who acts as a mediator between God and the world. He writes, *"To his Word, his chief messenger the Father of all has given the special prerogative, to stand on the border and separate the creature from the Creator."* And, *"of necessity was the **Logos** appointed as judge and **mediator**, who is called 'angel'."* And he speaks of *"God's firstborn, the Word, who holds the eldership among the angels, their ruler as it were."* But Philo really betrays the extent to which he has departed from his Jewish roots, and a proper understanding of the God of the Old Testament, when he calls the Word *"the second God, who is his Logos."* Again, **he is not speaking of Jesus** as there is no indication that he ever heard of Jesus!

Trinitarian Millard Erickson acknowledges the strong influence of Philo on **post** N.T. religious thinking. Regarding the *"Apologists,"* the church fathers of the late period before Nicea *(Justin Martyr, Tatian, Theophilus of Antioch, etc.)* and their attempt to offer a rational explanation of the relationship of Christ, *"the preexistent Son,"* to God the Father, he writes:

> *"In this explanation, they **drew heavily** on the concept of the **divine Logos or Word**. It was found in **later** Judaism and in Stoicism, and **through the influence of Philo it had become a fashionable cliche'**. The apologists' unique contribution was in drawing out the **further implication** of the concept" (p. 43).* Erickson says also: *"Ignatius' references to the Son deriving his sonship **from the conception in Mary's womb** should be thought of as simply a **common usage of theology** prior to Origen" (p. 40).* Please note: This Southern Baptist theologian says the idea of *"the Son deriving his **sonship** from **the conception in Mary's womb"***

was *"a common usage of theology **prior to Origen.**"* **After Origen** *(A.D. 185-254)* the non-biblical doctrine of Jesus' "eternal sonship" began to be taught. Notice carefully also: *"the concept of the **divine Logos**...through the influence of **Philo** had become a **fashionable cliche,**"* **before** Jesus. Wow! Listen to Erickson, *"the concept of the **divine Logos**...through the influence of **Philo** had become a **fashionable cliche,'** before Christ!"*

Regarding the teachings of Philo, Professor James Dunn says, *"Philo's thought, not least his concept of the **Logos**, is what can fairly be described as a unique synthesis* [combining] *of Platonic* [Plato] *and Stoic world-view with Jewish monotheism. The Logos seems to be envisaged as **a wholly independent being** who can act as intermediary between God and man."* He refers to Philo as a Jewish writer whose context of thought *"is strange and difficult"* and some of his allegories as *"strained and at times confusing or even contradictory."*

Remember, Philo had used the word *"logos"* (word) over 1400 times in his writings before the apostle John possibly had used it **once** in the first chapter of his gospel. Philo's tainted doctrine, corrupted by Greek philosophy, had already permeated Jewish thinking. It is easy to see how such language from the influential Philo as, ***"the mediating Logos,"*** or ***"the second God, who is his Logos,"*** when brought into Christianity, developed into the myth of Jesus as a **pre-existent divine being** distinct from God.

Thus, **Philo of Alexandria** helped to birth the school of thought that later produced **Athanasius of Alexandria** *(295-373 A.D.)*, the chief architect and proponent of the error that prevailed at Nicea; the idea that God existed in the form of two persons, *"That the Son is God, just as the Father is God."*

The *Encyclopedia Americana* says of Athanasius:
> *"**His teaching on the Logos furnished the basic ideas for the development of later Christological doctrine**" (Vol. 2; p. 603).*

The *Harper Collins Encyclopedia of Catholicism* says:
> *"**Trinitarian doctrine** as such emerged in the **fourth-century**, due largely to the efforts of Athanasius and the Cappadocians" (p. 1271).*

Trinitarian Professor Shirley C. Guthrie , Jr. writes in his best selling book *Christian Doctrine:*
> *"**The Bible does not teach the doctrine of the Trinity.** The language of the doctrine is the language of the ancient church **taken from classical Greek philosophy**" (p. 76-77). "**The doctrine of the Trinity is not found in the Bible**" (p. 80).* Again, *"...is the language of the ancient church* [not the N.T. church] **taken from classical Greek philosophy.** *"*

Listen to these words from Thomas Jefferson, third President of the United States and author of the Declaration of Independence:

> *"The Trinitarian idea triumphed in the church's creeds, not by the force of reason but by **the words of Athanasius**, and grew in the blood of thousands and thousands of martyrs."*

The strong influence that **Greek philosophy** had on the conclusions of Nicea is seen in the historical records of that gathering. The Emperor Constantine who had called the council of 300 bishops, and who presided over it from an exalted place on a wrought gold chair, gave an oration to this group in which he spoke with commendation of the Greek philosopher **Plato** *(427-347 B.C.)* whose teachings Philo followed, as having taught the doctrine of *"a second God,"* and *"the second deity proceeding from the first."* (Since when is Plato someone from whom Christians should derive their doctrine?)

Erickson states, *"**It is customary to assume that the major philosophical influence on the Greek** [Church] **fathers was Plato and the Stoics**" (p. 259).*

After Constantine spoke, the Council voted that **Jesus is God, just as the Father is God**, the second person of God! In their Platonic blindness they departed from the clear teaching of the O.T. regarding the Most High God being **one person**. (God calls Himself *"the Holy **One** of Israel"* twenty-six times in the book of Isaiah alone).

210

Is that what John meant, "A second God?"

>*"In the **beginning** was the Word and the Word was with God, and the Word was God. The same was in the beginning with God" (John 1:1-2).*

First, let's look at the word *"beginning."* One thing I have learned in my study of Scripture is, when you see the word *"beginning"* or the word *"end"* you have to ask the question, "Beginning of what?," or the "End of what?" For example, when Jesus said to his disciples, *"Ye have been with me from the beginning,"* he meant the beginning of his ministry, and not the beginning of time. When John says *"the devil sinneth from the beginning"* (I John 3:8), he meant from the **beginning of sin** and not from the devil's own beginning. (At the devil's own beginning he was sinless, *"the anointed cherub...perfect in thy ways from the day that thou was created, till iniquity was found in thee" Ezek. 28:14-15).* The apostle John uses the word *"beginning"* twenty-one times in his writings which is more than it is used by any other New Testament writer. **Not one time** when John uses the word *"beginning"* does he mean eternity past! So when he uses the word beginning in John 1:1, he is not speaking of the beginning of God: **God has no beginning!** He is not speaking of the beginning of eternity: **eternity has no beginning!** What "beginning?" Jesus answers this question himself in Revelation 3:14: *"These things saith the Amen, the faithful and true witness, the **beginning** of the creation of God."* The Greek word for **beginning** is the same in John 1:1 and Revelation 3:14. It is the Greek word *"arche"* and it means *"a commencement - **to commence in order of time."*** We need to stop reading John 1:1 as if it says, *"In **eternity past** was the Word..."* That is a mistaken idea! Jesus is the *"**beginning** of the creation of God,"* **first in order of time!** This agrees with what Paul said in Colossians 1:15: Jesus *"is the **image** of the invisible God, the **firstborn** of every **creature**,"* and *"the **image** of him* [God] *that **created him**" (3:10).* Neither John nor Paul nor any other New Testament writer thought or wrote of Jesus as a pre-existent, eternal being, **and certainly not as a "second person of God."**

Now what about the word *"Word"* that John used

"In the beginning was the Word, and the Word was with God..." (John 1:1). Remember, this was **not a second God** that was *"with God,"* so what was it?

If John used the Greek word *"logos,"* what did he mean? Note: The Old Testament was written in Hebrew and the New Testament has come to us in **Greek** manuscripts, whether or not the authors *wrote* in that language (more concerning this later). The Greek word *"**logos**" (Strong's Concordance #3056)* means *"**something said including the thought-motive-intent.**"* It is an *"**utterance.**"* In the beginning of creation **something was said!** This agrees with what John wrote also in his epistle of I John:

> *"That which was from the beginning, **which we have heard**...of the **Word** of life; For the life was manifested, and we have seen it, and bear witness, and show you **that eternal life, which was with the Father**, and was **manifested** unto*

us" *(I John 1:1-2).* Do you see the similarity between this and John chapter one?

So John says it was *"eternal life which was with the Father"* at the **beginning of creation**, and later manifested for us **through his Son**. Notice I John 5:11:

"And this is the record, that God hath given to us eternal life, and this life is in his Son."

"The book of life of the **Lamb slain from the foundation of the world**" *(Rev. 13:8).* That is, in the **thought, motive, intent,** and **utterance** of Almighty God. **So in the same reality in which Jesus existed before his birth, he was *"slain"* before his birth,** in the **plan, purpose** and **foreknowledge of God!**

This is why John wrote the *golden text* of the Bible, John 3:16:

*"For **God so loved** the world, that **he gave** his only begotten Son, that whosoever believeth in him should not perish, **but have everlasting life.**"*

It was also John who recorded Jesus' words from his great prayer to the Father in John 17:1-3:

*"Father...this is **life eternal**, that they might know thee **the only true God**, and Jesus Christ whom thou hast sent."*

Jesus and John knew what they wanted us to know: that there is only **one true God**, and no "second God," not even the Messiah *(the anointed one)* himself!

A biblical fact

Please see and understand this biblical fact. At the beginning of creation, before He ever created the first Adam whom He knew would fall through sin and take all of creation down with him, **God spoke** His Son, *"the last Adam...the second man" (I Cor. 15:45-47),* to redeem all of creation on an old rugged cross and *"condemn sin in the flesh" (Rom. 8:3).* **This is Jesus' part in creation.** He is redeemer of all of creation, **spoken before time, to come in time.** God not only spoke Jesus' birth, but He spoke his crucifixion, *"before the foundation of the world,"* and our salvation through him *"in the book of life from the foundation of the world." (Rev. 17:8).* Therefore Jesus could truly say in John 8:58, *"Before Abraham was, I am,"* since he was **spoken and real in the mind and purpose of God** from the "beginning."

> *"For since by man came death, by man came also the resurrection of the dead. For as in Adam all die, even so in Christ shall all be made alive. But every man in his own order: Christ the firstfruits; afterward they that are Christ's at his coming" (I Cor. 15:21-23).* All foreordained by God the Creator **before time,** to be manifested **in time.**

> *"But now **once** in the end of the world hath he
> [Jesus] appeared to put away sin by the sacrifice
> of himself" (Heb. 9:26).*

> *"But when the **fullness of time was come,** God
> sent forth his **Son, made of a woman,** made
> under the law" (Gal. 4:4).*

The Council of Nicea declared that Jesus is *"Begotten, **not made,**
of one substance with the Father,"* but many Scriptures including
the verse above, teach that he was *"made"* by God. *"His **Son,**
made of a woman."* Notice, **not just a body,** but God's *"Son"*
was *"**made of a woman!**"*

How were the worlds created?

> *"Through faith we understand that the worlds
> were framed by the **word of God**, [something
> said], so that things which are seen were not
> made of things which do appear" (Heb. 11:3).*

> *"By the **word of God** [something said], the
> heavens were of old, and the earth standing out
> of the water and in the water" (II Peter 3:5).*

> *"By the **word of the Lord** [something said] were
> the heavens made; and all the host of them by
> **the breath of his mouth**...For **he spoke**, and it
> was done, **he commanded**, and it stood fast"*

(Ps. 33:6, 9). Notice: *"word," "breath of his mouth," "he spoke."*

*"In the **beginning** God created the heavens and the earth" (Genesis 1:1).*

*"And **God said**, Let there be light" (v. 3).*

*"And **God said**, Let there be a firmament" (v. 6).*

*"And **God said**,...(v. 9); "And **God said**," (v. 11); "And **God said**," (v. 14); "And **God said**," (v. 20); "And **God said**," (v. 24).*

Properly understanding John

Now, with this in mind, we should be able to read John 1:1-2 with proper understanding.

"In the beginning was the logos ["something said, including the thought"], *and the **something said** was with God, and the **something said** was God"* [It was *"the breath of His mouth"*] *(Ps. 33:6).*

My friend, here is the most serious and devastating problem in Christian doctrine: Christians are guilty of confounding the Logos of Plato with John's use of the word *"logos"* for God's utterance or speech in John 1:1, and making of it a *"second Deity,"* i.e. a second person in the Trinity! **No two things in the world could be more different than Plato's *"Logos"* and John's *"logos!"***

The *Harper Collins Encyclopedia of Catholicism* says of the **Platonic** Christians who followed Philo:

> *"The **Platonists** [lovers and followers of Plato] of **Alexandria** conceived of the **Logos** as the **divine intermediary** between God and the world. Integrating these views, Philo (20 B.C. - A.D. 50) spoke of the **Logos** as the divine intention operating at the heart of creation. It is the power of creation and **the means through which we know God**. The early Church writers Ignatius of Antioch, Justin Martyr, Clement of Alexandria, and Athanasius **employed the notion of Logos** to shed light on **the mystery of God's** self-revelation in Jesus Christ (p. 792). In this fashion, while Philo's writings had but **minimal effect** on later Jewish thinking, **they became influential on the Church Fathers**, who preserved his writings for posterity."*

As we go forward we will prove that Philo had no affect on the writings of the beloved disciple John, an **unhellenized Galilean**, but he did have a devastating effect on the writings of the so called "Church Fathers," who themselves were "converted" Greek philosophers.

The famous twentieth century historian Will Durant, writes of Philo's concept of God and the divine Logos:

*"Fluctuating between **philosophy** and **theology**, between ideas and personifications, Philo sometimes thinks of **the Logos as a person**; in a poetic moment he calls the **Logos 'the first-begotten of God,' son of God by the virgin Wisdom**, and says that **through the Logos, God has revealed himself to man.** Since the soul is part of God, it can through reason rise to a mystic vision not quite of God, **but of the Logos. Philo's Logos was one of the most influential ideas in the history of thought.** Philo was a contemporary of Christ; **he apparently never heard of him; but he shared unknowingly in forming Christian theology.** The rabbis frowned upon his allegorical interpretations...they suspected the Logos doctrine was **a retreat from monotheism** [belief in One God]. But **the Fathers of the Church** admired the Jew's contemplative devotion, made abundant use of his allegorical principles to answer the critics of the Hebrew Scriptures, and joined with **Gnostics** and **Neo-Platonists** in accepting the **mystical vision of God"** (Caesar and Christ; p. 501-502),*

These ideas from Philo have absolutely no basis in Old Testament Scripture. Philo tells us he wrote these things *"in the heat of divine **possession**,"* when *"I knew not the **place**, or the **company**, or **myself, what I said or what I wrote.**"* This is an attempt by a

218

demon spirit to inject confusion into Jewish, and ultimately Christian, doctrine. And confusion it has brought. One thing is for certain: **we will never have favor with God, our prayers answered, and apostolic power, until we truly *"dehellenize"* Christianity and rid ourselves of these Greek concepts and doctrines!**

In what language did John the Apostle write?

Before we go further with our study of the word *"Word"* (logos) in John 1:1, we should attempt to answer the question as to what language John wrote in. I will make a statement at this point that cannot be successfully refuted. **There is no one on this planet who can prove that John ever took pen in hand and wrote the word *"logos."*** This is why.

No copies of John's original gospel are known to have survived to the present. The oldest fairly complete manuscripts of the New Testament, including John, in existence today are Codex Siniaticus and Codex Vaticanus, and date to about 350 A.D. They are both written in Greek. There is a fragment of John, also in Greek, that measures about two and a half by three and a half inches, containing five verses from chapter eighteen, that scholars have dated to about 150 A.D. Since it is commonly believed that John wrote his gospel between 85 and 90 A.D., it went through several copyings and possibly more than one translation before the making of the copies now in existence.

John probably wrote in the language best known to him, Aramaic. This beloved Apostle was a son of Galilee. Along with Peter and James, he was a poorly educated fisherman when Jesus called him to be a fisher of men. The high priest and his religious council according to Acts chapter four, *"saw the boldness of Peter and John, and perceived that they were unlearned and ignorant men" (v. 13).* John and Jesus spoke the language of Galilee, Aramaic, **not Greek**. Listen to the noted writer Philip Yancey:

> *"Speaking the common language of **Aramaic** in a slipshod way was a telltale sign of Galilean roots. The **Aramaic** words preserved in the Gospels **show that Jesus too, spoke in that northern dialect,** no doubt encouraging skepticism about him" (The Jesus I Never Knew; p. 60).*

Dr. Thomas McCall, Th. D., a noted theologian and authority on biblical languages, in his work, *The Language of The Gospel,* writes of the transition of the Jewish people from the Hebrew of the Old Testament to the Aramaic of New Testament times:

> *"The Jewish people learned to speak **Aramaic** in Babylon during the Babylonian captivity. When* [they] *returned to Israel, they carried back with them the language they had learned in Babylon. Hebrew was used in the synagogue when the Scriptures were read, but **the language of the street was Aramaic.** This continued through the time of **Christ,** and it is probable that **the language He most frequently used was the***

> ***common Aramaic.***" Again Dr. McCall refers to
> "*the language of Aramaic that **Jesus** and most of*
> *the people of Israel in His time spoke.*"

Concerning the language in which the Gospel of John is written, Professor Barry D. Smith of Crandall University states:

> "*The author seems to have written his gospel in **Aramaic** or a very Semitic type of Greek. The following is a list of grammatical features of John that most scholars agree suggest that the text is translated **Aramaic** or bears the influence of an author who **thought in Aramaic**...*" (The New Testament and Its Context; Crandall University; from their website).

Smith then lists six distinct Aramaic - Hebrew features of the Gospel of John which lead him to the following conclusion:

> "***These linguistic data suggest that the author's mother tongue was not Greek, but Aramaic.***"

So, it is likely that the apostle John wrote his gospel in the Aramaic language. Therefore he would not have used the Greek word "*logos*" in John 1:1, but rather the Aramaic word "*memra.*" This would match **the extensive use of "*memra*" in some of the Targums**, or Aramaic translations of the Old Testament commonly used in John's day by those Jews who spoke Aramaic.

John Gill in his, *Exposition of the Entire Bible,* at John 1:1, indicates that the meaning of John 1:1 is based on the meaning of *"memra" from the Targums* **rather than from the writings of Plato or his followers**. The general meaning of the Aramaic word *"memra"* is *"speech,"* *"utterance,"* or *"word."*

The *Pulpit Commentary*, a well known and widely used commentary says of these meanings:

> *"The New Testament writers never use the term* [logos] *to denote reason, or thought, or self consciousness, but always denote by it **speech, utterance,** or **word**....."* *(St. John; Vol. 1).*

Every other verse in the Bible endorses the fact that John meant this:

> *"In the beginning* [some certain beginning] *was the word* [something said]*, and the **something said** was with God, and the **something said** was God"* [the breath of His mouth] *(John 1:1).*

Consider this statement by the **trinitarian**, Professor James Dunn:

> *"But if we translated **logos** as **God's utterance** instead, it would become clearer that the poem* [John's Prologue] *did not necessarily intend the **Logos** in verses 1-13 **to be thought of as a personal divine being**"* *(Christology In The Making; p. 243).*

If we make *"Word"* the pre-existent *being* of Greek philosophy, rather than God's utterance, the *"breath of His mouth" (Ps. 33:6)*, we create for ourselves many dilemmas. Listen to **trinitarian** Millard Erickson:

> **"Here is the seeming contradiction of the Word being God, and yet not being God."**

My friend, the importance of understanding John 1:1 cannot be overstated. Because, upon a misunderstanding and misinterpretation of this verse a huge doctrinal structure has been built for 1700 years that is without foundation, and God is about to bring it down. Without inserting the Greek Logos into John 1:1, Christianity has no basis for its doctrine of the Trinity. Listen again to Professor Erickson:

> *"We would **seem to have** in this **one verse** possibly the strongest intimation* ["a hint; indirect suggestion"] *of the **Trinity** found anywhere in Scripture."* He continues, *"however, there are several other places where **at least subconsciously John appears to be wrestling** with issues that **eventually led the church to formulate the doctrine of the Trinity.**"* **Wow! Incredible!**

So it is likely that John wrote in his common language the Aramaic word *"memra,"* and **never in his life** penned the Greek word *"logos."* **This of course makes mute** the discussion by some Christian scholars as to **why John chose to use "logos," a word**

that had already been given a meaning that is foreign to the Old Testament, the teachings of Jesus, and the writings of all of the New Testament writers.

Trinitarian scholars Roger Olson and Christopher Hall, writing in their book, *The Trinity,* struggle with this possible use of the word *"logos"* in John 1:1, 14:

> *"How could the logos become a human being?* **John wisely does not attempt to explain how such could be the case.** *Apart from the events of the gospel narrative itself,* **John would never have pictured God in such a complex manner**" (p. 7).

If John Wrote The Word "Logos"

It has been over nineteen hundred years since John wrote his gospel, and again no original manuscripts of his are known to be in existence; therefore no one knows for sure if he wrote *"logos"* in his prologue. However, if he did, he for sure did not follow Socrates, Plato, and Philo in their Greek philosophic meaning of the word. That fact we have proven! Whichever word he used, *"memra"* or *"logos,"* he meant *utterance, speech, word.* Here are **three witnesses** from the Bible that prove it.

> *"By the* **word of the Lord** *were the heavens made; and all the host of them by the* **breath of his mouth**...For **he spoke**, *and it was done"* *(Psalms 33:6, 9).* Note: *"In the* **beginning God created**..." *(Gen. 1:1).* *"And* **God said**..." *(v. 3, 6, 9, 11, 14, 20, 24).*

*"Through faith we understand that the worlds were framed by the **word of God**"* [something said] *(Heb. 11:3).*

*"By the **word of God**,* [something said] *the heavens were of old, and the earth..." (II Peter 3:5).*

The Word of God in the Old Testament

Anyone who has read much of the Jewish Scriptures which we call the *"Old Testament"* is familiar with the phrase *"the word of God."* This occurs more than 240 times, and over 90% of these references describe a word of prophecy (never a person). The phrase is more or less a term for the prophetic claim that the prophet expresses the authoritative revelation and will of God in a particular situation. Thus we read again and again *"the word of the Lord."* Consider these examples:

*"After these things **the word of the Lord** came unto Abram in a vision, saying, Fear not, Abram" (Gen. 15:1).*

*"He that feared **the word of the Lord** among the servants of Pharaoh..." (Ex. 9:20).*

*"If Balak would give me his house full of silver and gold, I cannot go beyond **the word of the Lord my God**"* [Balaam] *(Num. 22:18).*

*"And the woman said to Elijah, Now by this I know that thou art a man of God, and that **the word of the Lord in thy mouth** is truth" (I Kings 17:24).*

*"And it came to pass the same night, that **the word of Lord** came to Nathan, saying..." (I Chron. 17:3).*

So, in each of the above instances, and over two hundred more, *"the word of the Lord"* (or *"God"*), is His message *to* or *through* His chosen prophet. However, in a few verses in the Old Testament, God's *"word"* is spoken of in a way that seems to give it an independent existence of its own. Please consider the following:

*"**He sent his word**, and healed them, and delivered them from their destructions" (Ps. 107:20).*

*"**He sendeth forth his commandment** upon earth: **his word runneth** very swiftly" (Ps. 147:15).*

*"**The Lord sent a word** into Jacob, and it hath lighted upon Israel" (Isa. 9:8).*

*"So shall **my word** be that goeth forth out of my mouth: **it shall not return unto me void**, but it shall accomplish that which I please, and it shall*

*prosper in the thing whereto **I sent it**" (Isa. 55:11).*

So the powerful *"word of God,"* once uttered, has as it were, a life of its own, especially as written down, when it functions as Torah or Scripture. But for these prophets, the word they spoke under divine inspiration was no independent entity separate from God Himself. On the contrary, it was precisely the word of God, the utterance and breath of God, **God himself speaking**. Please notice:

> *"**By the word of the Lord** were the heavens made; and all the host of them by **the breath of his mouth**. For **he spoke**, and it was done; **he commanded**, and it stood fast" (Ps. 33:6, 9).*

As Professor Dunn says, *"It is an error to see in such personifications an approach to **personalization**. Nowhere either in the Bible or in the extra-canonical literature of the Jews is the word of God **a personal agent or on the way to become such**" (Christology In The Making; p. 219).* So why did Philo, this famous Hellenistic Jewish writer from **Alexandria, Egypt,** not understand that? Again, he was blinded by his love for and fascination with, Plato and Greek philosophy. And he was just as obsessed with the *"divine Logos"* as Socrates and the Stoics before him. Listen to Professor Dunn:

> *"There can be no doubt of the importance of the word **logos** for Philo - he uses it more than 1400 times in his extant writings. Philo quite often*

> *speaks of the Logos as though a real being* **distinct from God**, *who acts as intermediary* **between** *God and the world."*

It is for sure that the Greek church fathers, **after the deaths of the Apostles,** followed this erroneous Platonic doctrine of the *"divine Logos,"* and applied it **falsely** to Messiah Jesus. But to claim that **the apostle John** followed Heraclitus, Socrates, Plato, the Stoics, and Philo in their understanding of the Creator and His dealings with the world, is a major insult to him and to the Holy God who anointed him to write!

The "Word of God" in the New Testament

Although it is probable that the New Testament was written in Aramaic, the two oldest known manuscripts date from about 350 A.D. and are in the Greek language. Therefore we will deal with it on that basis. The Greek word for *"word"* or *"utterance,"* as in the *"word of God"* is *"logos."* It occurs 331 times in the New Testament and its uses vary within the basic meaning.

Some examples of these uses are: communication *(Matt. 5:37)*, utterance *(Matt. 12:32; 15:12; Luke 20:20)*, question *(Matt. 21:24)*, command *(Luke 4:36)*, report, information and rumor *(Matt. 28:15; Mark 1:45; Luke 5:15; Acts 11:22)*, discourse *(Matt. 15:12)*, wording *(I Cor. 15:2)*, word of mouth *(Acts 15:27; II Cor. 10:10)*, as apposed to the written word *(Acts 1:1)*, mere words contrasted with power and action *(I Thess. 1:5; I Cor. 4:19)*, a matter *(Mark 9:10; Acts 8:21)*, words of Scripture *(I Cor. 15:54)*, words of warning *(Heb. 5:11)*, give account *(Rom. 14:12)*,

228

settlement of an account *(Phil. 4:15)*, motive *(Acts 10:29)*, proclamation, teaching, instruction *(Luke 4:32; 10:39; John 4:41; 17:20)*; and also the word of God, the word of the Lord, the word of promise, of truth, of life, the word of Jesus, and the word concerning Jesus. To the Apostles the *"word"* was the message **about Jesus**, but never Jesus **incarnated!** In only **two** of these 331 occurrences of *"logos"* or *"word,"* do even trinitarian scholars think they see it *"incarnated"* as a **person** in Jesus Christ, as opposed to what the *"word"* or *"utterance"* of God produced or generated in the womb of the virgin Mary. Those two places are John 1:1, and 14.

Jesus and The "Word of God"

When Jesus preached or taught, **he spoke the *"word of God."*** You might ask, how can this be true if he was not God Himself? Let Jesus tell us:

> *"My doctrine is not mine, but **his that sent** me. If any man will do **his will**, he shall know of the doctrine, whether it be **of God**, or whether I speak of myself" (John 7:16-17).*

> *"...I do nothing of myself; but **as my Father hath taught me, I speak** these things" (John 8:28).*

> *"For I have not spoken of myself; but the Father which sent me, **he gave me a commandment, what I should say, and what I should speak**...whatsoever I speak therefore, **even as the***

Father said unto me, so I speak" *(John 12:49-*
50). Note: The above statements were recorded
by the Apostle John.

Jesus also spoke **about** the *"word"* of God. Please notice his
words:

> *"The sower soweth the **word**. And these are they*
> *by the wayside, where the **word** is sown; but*
> *when they have **heard**, Satan cometh*
> *immediately, and taketh away the **word** that was*
> ***sown** in their hearts. And these are they likewise*
> *which are sown on stony ground; who when they*
> *have **heard the word**, immediately receive **it** with*
> *gladness... . And these are they which are sown*
> *among thorns; such as **hear the word**, and the*
> *cares of this world, and the deceitfulness, and*
> *the lusts of other things entering in, **choke the***
> ***word**, and **it** becometh unfruitful. And these are*
> *they which are sown on good ground; such as*
> ***hear the word**, and receive **it**, and bring forth*
> *fruit..."* *(Mark 4:14-20)*.

The above verses are very important to our understanding as to
how Jesus perceived himself in regard to the *"word"* of God. He
cannot have seen himself as the *"word incarnate."* To Jesus the
"word" is something that is *"sown,"* that is *"heard,"* that Satan
"taketh away," that is called *"it,"* and can be *"choked."* This can
be God's *"words,"* His *"gospel,"* and the *"preaching concerning*
Jesus," but **it cannot be "Jesus!"** No New Testament writer,

230

including John, quotes Jesus as saying or even hinting that he himself is the *"word* [logos] *of God"* **in fleshly form!** Jesus claimed to be and is, *"the **way**, the **truth**, and the **life**,"* but he never once claimed to be ***"the word!"***

How Jesus saw himself!

> *"But now ye seek to kill me, a **man** [Greek - anthropos - Strongs #444 **"a human being"**] that hath told you the truth which I have heard of God" (John 8:40).*

> *"The woman saith unto him, I know that **Messiah** cometh, which is called Christ:...Jesus saith unto her, **I that speak unto thee am he"** (John 4:25-26).*

A human being! The Messiah, anointed one of God! These are Jesus' claims for himself, and God has authorized **no one**, not me-you-or anyone else- to disagree with Jesus!

Understanding John 1:3

Now lets look at John 1:3, which says in the King James Version of the Bible, first published in 1611 A.D.:

> *"All things were made by **him**; and without **him** was not any thing made that was made."*

Is the word *"him"* in this verse translated properly? First of all it does not fit with a true understanding of the two preceding verses.

231

("Something said" is not a "him"). Second, it is important to note that of nine prominent English translations that **preceded** the King James Version, not one used the word *"him."* **Eight** of the nine rendered John 1:3, *"By **it** all things were made. Without **it** nothing was made" (Tyndale Bible, 1535; Matthew, 1535; Tavener, 1539; The Great (Cranmer's) Bible, 1539; Whittingham, 1557; Genera, 1560; Bishop's Bible, 1568; Tomson NT, 1607).* **One**, the famous Coverdale Bible of 1550 has *"the same"* rather than "it." **None of these nine say *"him."*** Why did the King James translators render *"it"* as *"him,"* as if it were a person? (They also gave *"word"* a capital *"W"* as if it were a person, which many other translators did not do). They were trinitarians and their mistaken doctrine overpowered their sense of scholarship. They had been influenced by Plato, Philo, the Nicean Council, and 1300 years of false Roman Catholic tradition. Their error has helped to lead millions of sincere Christians astray in their understanding of who the one true God is! Please consider:

In 1582 Gregory Martin did a Latin to English translation, the **Roman Catholic Douay-Rheims** version, in which he became the **first** to render John 1:3, *"All things were made by **him**."* When the King James translators, themselves trinitarians, approached John 1:3, **although the Greek does not say this**, they followed Martin and rendered it, *"All things were made by **him**."* This mistaken translation caused people to believe that the *"Son of God"* created the universe and was also *"God,"* causing the confusion that we have been dealing with throughout the pages of this book. From Tyndale's translation in 1526 until today, there have been at least **fifty notable translations** that did not follow

232

Douay and the KJV in their serious error. The following twenty-nine versions specifically say *"it."*

1. *"All things were made by it"* (Tyndale, 1526)
2. *"All things were made by it and without it nothing was made"* (Matthews' Bible, 1537)
3. *"All things were made by it and without it was made nothing that was made"* (The Great Bible, 1539)
4. *"All things were made by it"* (Taverner NT, 1540)
5. *"All things were made by it"* (Whittingham, 1557)
6. *"All things were made by it"* (The Geneva Bible, 1560)
7. *"All things were made by it"* (Bishops' Bible, 1568)
8. *"All things were made by it"* (Tomson NT, 1607)
9. *"Nor can anything be produced that has been made without it [Reason]"* (John LeClerc, 1701)
10. *"In the beginning was Wisdom...All things were made by it"* (Wakefield NT, 1791)
11. *"The Word...All things were made by it"* (Alexander Campbell, founder of the Church of Christ, 1826)
12. *"The Word...All things were formed by it"* (Dickinson, A New and Corrected Version of the NT, 1833)
13. *"All things were made by it"* (Barnard, 1847)
14. *"Through it [the logos] everything was done"* (Wilson, Emphatic Diaglott, 1864)
15. *"All things through it arose into being"* (Folsom, 1869)
16. *"All things were made through it"* (Sharpe, Revision of the Authorized English Version, 1898)

17. *"All things came into being in this God-conception and apart from **it** came not anything into being that came into being"* (Overbury, 1925)

18. *"All came into being through **it**"* (Knoch, 1926)

19. *"Without **it** nothing created sprang into existence"* (Johannes Greber, 1937)

20. *"**It** was in the beginning with God, by **its** activity all things came into being"* (Martin Dibelius, The Message of Jesus Christ, translated by F.C. Grant, 1939)

21. *"Through **its** agency all things came into being and apart from **it** has not one thing come to be"* (William Temple, Archbishop of Canterbury, Readings from St. John's Gospel, 1939)

22. *"All was done through **it**"* (Tomanek, 1958)

23. *"**It** was his last werd. Ony **it** come first"* (Gospels in Scouse, 1977)

24. *"By **it** everything had being, and without **it** nothing had being"* (Schonfield, The Original NT, 1985)

25. *"In the beginning was the Plan of Yahweh. All things were done according to **it**"* (Hawkins, Book of Yahweh, 1987)

26. *"All things happened through **it**"* (Gaus, Unvarnished NT, 1991)

27. *"In the beginning was the divine word and wisdom...everything came to be by means of **it**"* (Robert Miller, The Complete Gospels, Annotated Scholars' Version, 1992)

28. *"In the beginning there was the divine word and wisdom, everything came into being by means of **it**"* (Robert Funk, The Five Gospels, 1993)

29. *"In the beginning was the **message**, through **it** all things were done"* (Daniels, The Four Gospels: A Non-Ecclesiastical NT, 1996)

The foregoing are twenty-nine credible witnesses that the apostle John did not believe the *"word"* to be a **person**, the *"incarnate"* Son of God.

Regarding John 1:10

> *"He was in the world, and the world was made **by** him, and the world knew him not."*

Jesus never claimed that the world was made *"**by**"* him. Again and again he declared that God his Father was the Creator *(Matt. 19:4-6; Mark 10:6; 13:19; Luke 12:28).* At the time of creation it was in God's plan to redeem it back to Himself **through** the sinless sacrifice of His Son Jesus, on Calvary. Therefore *Today's English Version*, the *NIV*, the *Jerusalem Bible*, the *NASB*, the *RSV*, *God's Word Translation*, the *Holman CSB*, and the *New King James* are far more accurate when they render John 1:10 as, the world was made *"**through him**."*

What John meant in John 1:14 (Christianity must get this right!) With the foregoing in mind, we are able to read what John wrote in verse fourteen with clear biblical understanding:

> *"And the word-memra-logos* [utterance, speech, something said] *was made flesh* [Jesus]*, and dwelt among us, (and we beheld his glory, the*

> *glory as of the only begotten of the Father), full of grace and truth.* " **What God said became flesh!**

John for sure did not write nor intend for us to believe that:

> *"In **eternity past** was the **Son**, and the **Son** was with God, and the **Son** was God.* " **That is not what he says!**

Not only in John but throughout the New Testament there is no pre-existing Son. God spoke in Old Testament times *"unto the fathers by the prophets" (Heb. 1:2)*, not by a Son. Angels of God were not instructed to worship the Son until he was *"brought forth into the world" (Heb. 1:6).* In reality there was no Son of God until that time, because the *"Son"* of God was to be a descendant of David *(II Sam. 7:14-16).* According to Hebrews 1:5, God said regarding His *"Son,"* some nine hundred years **before** his birth in Bethlehem *(II Samuel 7:14)*:

> *"I **will be** to him a Father, and he **shall be** to me a Son.* "

Yes, Jesus Christ is the supernaturally conceived, virgin-born, sinless Son of God; savior, redeemer, Messiah, and the destined one-thousand-year ruler of planet Earth. But he never claimed to be *"God,"* or the pre-existent second person of a triune God that moved into the womb of Mary and came forth impersonating a baby. Neither did his chosen Apostles and the inspired Bible writers claim this for him. Listen to his apostle Peter to whom the *"Father which is in heaven"* had given special revelation on this subject:

236

Mark 12:29 *"Thou art that **Christ**."*

Luke 9:20 *" The **Christ** of God."*

*"Christ...who verily was **foreordained** [Note: not "pre-existent"] before the foundation of the world, but was manifest in these last times for you..." (I Peter 1:19-20).*

Every other verse in the Bible is a witness to this truth, and these statements by Peter never were corrected or amended by Jesus, John, Paul or any other writer of Holy Scripture. Here is a question for you dear reader. Who do **you** say that Jesus is? There could hardly be a more important question than this, since the apostle Paul warned of the danger of preaching *"**another Jesus**, whom we have not preached" (II Cor. 11:4)*, rather than the one all of Holy Scripture so clearly portrays. We must be sure we are believing in and preaching the **Jesus of the Bible**, and not a Jesus of mistaken tradition (i.e. an Incarnated Jesus!).

Conclusion
In this and the preceding chapters we have looked at statements from Holy Scripture, encyclopedias, historians, and Trinitarian scholars, credible sources that can help us understand how Christianity arrived at its erroneous doctrine about God; doctrine that preaches God as one-third of who He is, that preaches Christ to the exclusion of the Father, and gives the awesome Creator's

glory to His virgin-born, human Son. Regarding the *"glory"* that is due God and Jesus, we were so occupied with a supposed *"Incarnation"* in John 1:14, that we failed to see an indication of what might be Christianity's greatest error, **the limits of Jesus' glory!** Notice carefully: *"...and we beheld **his glory**, the glory as of **the only begotten of the Father**... ."*

That is Jesus' glory! The one and only time that God our Father has birthed a child from the womb of a virgin by a creative act of His Spirit, is in the case of our Lord Jesus Messiah. If we give Jesus additional glory, such as making him the *"creator of all,"* the *"eternal God,"* *"God the Son co-equal and co-eternal with the Father,"* or *"the King of heaven,"* we have robbed God our Father of the glory that He alone demands and deserves!

Based on these biblical as well as historical facts, it is time for Christianity to acknowledge the pagan origins of its doctrines of the Trinity and the Incarnation, repent, and purge itself of these demon-inspired and promoted teachings, that diminish the work that Jesus did of condemning *"sin in the flesh,"* and rob God our Father of His glory!

Listen to the *Harper Collins Encyclopedia of Catholicism* on Incarnation:

> *"This **notion** can be understood to refer to the moment when **God became a human being** at the conception of Jesus in his mother, Mary."*

The pagan origins of *"incarnation"* through the divine Logos doctrine are stated well by historian Will Durant:

> *"Philo's Logos was one of the most influential ideas in the history of thought. Its antecedents* [to precede] *in **Heraclitus, Plato**, and the **Stoics** are **obvious**. Philo was a contemporary of Christ; he apparently never heard of him; **but he shared unknowingly in forming Christian theology**" (Caesar and Christ; p. 502).*

Also by Professor Simon Blackburn:

> *"Philo allowed himself allegorical interpretations of the Judaic scriptures, bringing their message as closely as possible into harmony with this version of the **Platonic** world view. **Platonism** thereby became the **background philosophical underpinning** of the theologies of the monotheistic religions" (Plato's Republic: A Biography; p. 105).*

And in these shocking statements from the *Global Encyclopedia*:

> *"**Incarnation denotes the embodiment of a deity in human form**. The idea occurs frequently in **mythology**. In ancient times, certain kings and priests, were often thought to be divinities. In **Hinduism**, Vishnu* [the second person of the Hindu trinity] *is believed to have taken **nine incarnations**. For **Christians**, the incarnation is*

a central dogma referring to the belief that the **eternal Son of God***, the second person of the Trinity, became man in the person of Jesus Christ.* **The incarnation was defined as a doctrine only after long struggles by early church councils.** *The Council of Nicea (325) defined* **the deity of Christ***...; the Council of Constantinople (381) defined* **the full humanity of the incarnate Christ***...; and the Council of Chalcedon (451) defined* **the two natures of Christ,** *divine and human" (Vol. 11; p. 73).*

The "Word" brought to Mary

From our study of the Bible we can conclude that something similar to this happened just over 2000 years ago. The Lord God called the angel Gabriel into His throne room and gave him a very special assignment, he was to deliver the **word of God** to Nazareth! (Notice Gabriel's words in Luke 1:19, *"I am Gabriel, that stands in the* **presence** *of God, and am sent to* **speak** *unto thee..."*). He was told to find a virgin named Mary, and tell her that she was *"highly favored,"* and *"the Lord is with thee,"* and that *"thou hast found favor with* **God***."* She was to be told of a **miraculous conception** that would take place in her womb, by *"the power of the Highest,"* and for this reason precisely, the holy child *"which shall be born of thee shall be called the* **Son** *of God."*

Gabriel did as he was told and delivered the **word of God** to Mary! And what was her response? *"Be it unto me according to thy word."* So Mary received the spoken *"word of God,"* God's utterance, into herself, and it produced a real human baby, the unique, sinless Son of God!

I once was blind but now I see.

Thank God for Jesus!

*"We have observed that the specific metaphysical vehicle used to express **the classical doctrine of the Trinity** as originally formulated was a **Greek metaphysics** that was viable in that time but no longer makes a great deal of sense to most persons today. While it is customary to assume that the **major philosophical influence** on the Greek [church] fathers was **Plato** and the **Stoics**, [Michael] Durrant believes the influence of **Aristotle** should not be overlooked."*

(Trinitarian scholar Millard J. Erickson; Southern Baptist)

---

*"**The Bible does not teach the doctrine of the Trinity.** Neither the word 'trinity' itself nor such language as 'one-in-three,' 'one essence' (or 'substance'), and '**three persons**' is biblical language. The language of the doctrine is the language of the ancient church **taken from classical Greek philosophy.**"*

(Trinitarian professor Shirley C. Guthrie, Jr.; *Christian Doctrine*)

Chapter 32

Checking Our Doctrine And Worship

T here is a passage in Paul's letter to the Galatians, chapter two, verses one and two, that the Holy Spirit recently brought to my attention and it impacted me greatly! Paul says:

> *"Then fourteen years after I went up again to Jerusalem with Barnabas, and took Titus with me also. And I went up by revelation, and communicated unto them that gospel which I preach among the Gentiles, but privately to them which were of reputation, **lest by any means I should run, or had run, in vain"** (Galatians 2:1, 2 KJV).*

What these verses are saying to us is that the great apostle Paul, after at least fourteen years of ministry, went to visit the other Apostles in Jerusalem and presented his doctrine for their examination, *"lest by any means I should run, or had run in vain."* Winston Churchill said, *"Courage is what it takes to stand up and speak; courage is also what it takes to sit down and listen."* Paul listened! Look at Today's English Version of verse two:

> *"I went because God revealed to me that I should go. In a private meeting with the leaders, I explained to them the gospel message that I preach to the Gentiles. **I did not want my work in the past or in the present to go for nothing."***

243

Wow! Such humility! Some people just do not have what it takes to admit that they have been mistaken in their beliefs. But Paul knew the importance of getting our doctrine right!

> *"Examine yourselves, whether ye be in the faith; prove your own selves" (2 Cor. 13:5).*

The word "faith" in the verse above is *"pistis"* in the Greek, and it means correct religious *"persuasion."* Proper belief! Paul knew that the judgement day to come would **try with fire** every person's life and ministry.

> *"According to the grace of God which is given unto me, as a wise masterbuilder, I have laid the foundation, and another buildeth thereon. But let every man take heed how he buildeth thereupon. Now if any man build upon this foundation **gold, silver, precious stones, wood, hay, stubble;** Every man's work shall be made manifest: for the day shall declare it, because it shall be revealed by fire; **and the fire shall try every man's work of what sort it is**. If any man's work **abide** which he hath built thereupon, **he shall receive a reward**. If any man's work shall be burned, **he shall suffer loss**: but he himself shall be saved; yet so as by fire"(1Corinthians 3:10, 12-15).*

What an awesome and sad statement! *"...he shall suffer loss* (of reward): *but he himself shall be saved."* Saved...but lose his reward! Look at this statement from Jesus:

244

> *"Whosoever therefore shall break one of these*
> ***least*** *commandments,* ***and shall teach men so****, he*
> *shall be called the* ***least in the kingdom of***
> ***heaven...****"(Matthew 5:19).*

Remember, Jesus taught that the **greatest** commandment is, *"Listen...God is* ***one Lord.****"* If teachers who teach wrong concerning the *"least"* command *"shall be called least in the kingdom of heaven"*, what will be the state of those who teach men wrong regarding this *"greatest"* of commandments, saying that God is "**three** persons in a Trinity". They will suffer **great loss** when they stand before God! *"**HE SHALL SUFFER LOSS**....... ."* That is why the apostle James says:

> *"My brothers! Not many of you should become*
> *teachers, because you know that **we teachers** will*
> *be judged with **greater strictness than others***"
> *(James 3:1 Today's English Version).*

A doctrine built on "hints"

After my first book, *To God Be The Glory,* was published in 2006, proclaiming One Eternal God, the Father, who has a supernaturally conceived, virgin-born, human Son, our savior, the Messiah Jesus, someone challenged me with a book titled, *Renewal Theology*, by Trinitarian scholar J. Rodman Williams. Chapter four is *The Holy Trinity*, and begins: *"We come now to the **central mystery** of the Christian faith - the doctrine of the Holy Trinity, or the doctrine of the Triune God."* This first paragraph ends, *"**The Christian faith is faith in the Triune God.**"*

And on what, according to Brother Williams, is this **foundational** faith of Christianity, *"faith in the Triune God,"* based? He writes:

> *"In the Old Testament there is **no distinct** **reference** to God as **existing in three persons**. **Hints** of it, however, may be found"* (p. 84). *"Elohim is a plural noun, and though **no clear** **statement of a trinity is contained**, a plurality of persons **may** well be **implied**"* (p. 85). *"**No** **trinity of persons** as such **is declared**, but the **idea of plurality seems** to be definitely **suggested**"* [*"definitely suggested?"*] (p. 85). *"...hence there is the **suggestion** of a **second, alongside God**"* (p. 85). *"Although these passages **do not specifically depict** one God in three persons, **they point in that direction**"* (p. 85). *"The Spirit is not here said to be a **person**, though it can be **inferred**"* (p. 85). *"**It is the** **Christian claim** that **all three** of these persons are God"* (p. 87). *"This unquestionably **implies** divinity for the Son"* (p. 87). *"There are many other texts that **without directly using the** **terminology of 'the Son'** speak of Jesus Christ as God"* (p. 88). *"Although it could be argued that Jesus is not talking about **an eternal** **procession**, such would seem to be **implied**"* (Renewal Theology; Zondervan; p. 93).

Is this what the *"foundational"* doctrine of the Trinity is based on? The doctrine which a person must whole-heartedly believe or else be lost? Such words as *"hints," "implied," "suggested," "do not specifically depict," "inferred,"* and *"would **seem to be implied?"*** In all, this trinitarian theologian and doctor of the church uses the words *hints, implied, suggested* or *inferred* (or their derivatives) **nine times** in this one chapter, in an effort to prove the existence of a Triune God. (Remember his statement, *"**The Christian faith is faith in the Triune God."***)

I would not at all question Brother Williams' sound character or good intentions, but his use of such phrases as *"definitely suggested"* and *"unquestionably implies"* is characteristic of Trinitarian and Oneness double-talk in general. Other examples we hear are *"God-man," "God the Son," "One God in three persons," "fully God and fully man,"* and *"triune God."*

Please ask yourself these questions. Is God a God who *"hints"*? Does he just *"imply"* regarding serious matters? Are the *Ten Commandments* actually just ten *"suggestions?"* No way! The true doctrines of God's Holy Bible are clearly stated. Anything else will not stand the **trial by fire** on judgement day!

What the Apostles taught about God
We don't have Paul and the other Apostles with us today so that we might present our doctrine to them for scrutiny, but we do have their inspired writings so we can carefully examine it ourselves. Consider these biblical facts.

- Paul said "God" 513 times in his thirteen epistles, and not once can it be proven that he was speaking of Jesus Messiah; it was always the **Father**!

- Peter said "God" 46 times in his two epistles, and not once was he referring to Jesus; it was always the **Father**!

- James, the half brother of Jesus, said "God" 17 times in his epistle, and not once was he referring to Jesus; it was always the **Father**! (Note: The focus of this book isn't who Jesus is not, but who God our Father is).

Paul was very clear in his teaching about God. For example:

*"Blessed be the **God and Father** of our Lord Jesus Christ...(Ephesians 1:3).*

*"Now a mediator is not a mediator of one, but **God is one**" (Galatians 3:20).*

*"For there is **one God**, and one mediator between God and men, the man Christ Jesus..." (1 Timothy 2:5).*

*"**One God** and Father of all, who is above all, and through all, and in you all" (Ephesians 4:6).*

"Now unto the King [God the Great King] *eternal, immortal, invisible, **the only wise God**,*

248

> *be honour and glory for ever and ever. Amen" (I*
> *Timothy 1:17).*

Perhaps at this point we could invite the apostle Paul into our discussion for his best definition of "God". Listen carefully to him:

> *"... we know that an idol is nothing in the world,*
> *and that there is **none other God but one**. For*
> *though there be that are called gods, **whether in***
> ***heaven** [Note: "whether in heaven"] or in earth,*
> *(as there be gods many, and lords many,) But to*
> *us there is but **one God,** the **Father**, of whom are*
> *all things, and we **in him**; and one Lord Jesus*
> *Christ, by whom are all things, and we by him.*
> *Howbeit there is not in every man that*
> *knowledge..." (1 Corinthians 8:4-7).* Notice:
> *"But **to us** there is but **one God**, the **Father**,... ."*
>
> *"But **to us** there is but **one God**, the **Father**,... ."*
>
> *"But **to us** there is but **one God**, the **Father**,... ."*

My friend, if something in your spirit rebels against that clear statement by Paul, you should check your doctrine!

Paul Never Taught An Incarnation

The crux of the whole matter regarding whether Jesus is *"God,"* *"God the Son,"* or rather in fact the **human Son of God** comes down to this question, What really happened in Mary's womb?

Was the birth of Jesus an **incarnation**, or a **miraculous conception**? *Webster's* says *"incarnation"* means (1) *"endowment with a human body,"* (2) *"any person or animal serving as the embodiment of a god or spirit."* Incarnation is not a biblical concept but rather a **pagan** one. Greek and Roman mythology are full of gods becoming men, and in Hindu teaching the second person of the *"Hindu trinity,"* Vishnu, has been *incarnated* as a human nine times. The respected *Harper-Collins Bible Dictionary* says:

> (Incarnation) *"refers to the Christian doctrine that the pre-existent Son of God became man in Jesus. None of these writers* (Matthew, Mark, Luke) *deals with the question of Jesus' pre-existence. Paul does not directly address the question of the incarnation... . **It is only with the fathers of the church in the third and fourth centuries, that a full-fledged theory of the incarnation develops"*** (*p. 452-453*).

To Paul, Jesus God's *"Son"*, was *"made **of** a woman"(Gal. 4:4)*. Note: Not "made **before** the woman." Paul taught that Jesus is the *"second man...the last Adam" (I Cor. 15:45-47)*. He preached to the Greeks on Mars' hill in Acts seventeen regarding God the Creator of all, and, *"**that man** whom he* [God] *hath ordained" (v. 31)*.

To the inspired writer of Hebrews *"it is evident that our **Lord** sprang* [arose] *out of Juda" (Heb. 7:14)*. The apostle Peter, to whom the "Father which is in heaven" gave a definite revelation as to who Jesus is, believed that Christ *"verily was **foreordained** [not pre-existent] before the foundation of the world, but was manifest in these last times..." (I Peter 1:20).*

Please give serious consideration to the following questions. Did Almighty God shrink Himself "down-down-down" to a single cell and move into the womb of a virgin, causing Mary to carry the Eternal God around in her womb, as most Oneness Christians believe? Did "God the Son", the "second person of the Trinity", a pre-existent, eternal being move into Mary's womb and come out looking like a baby, as most Trinitarian Christians teach? The two above mentioned groups scoff at the **obviously false** doctrine taught by the Jehovah's Witnesses, who believe that Michael the Archangel was **incarnated** in Mary's womb, not realizing that they teach doctrines that are almost as ridiculous.

The following statements by some prominent Christian ministers whom I love and pray for, will illustrate my point very well!

Dr. David Reagan, the respected minister and Bible teacher of *Lamb & Lion Ministries* posted an article in the Nov.-Dec. 2010 issue of his *Lamplighter* magazine titled, *The Mystery of The Incarnation*, which states:

> *"He who is **Almighty** became a **suckling baby**. He who is **all wise** took on the **dumbness** of a newborn. **He whom the heavens cannot contain was enclosed in a woman's womb**. He who is infinite became a **microscopic cell**. He who is*

the Creator became a creature. **He who is light was entombed for nine months in warm darkness.** *Can there be a greater mystery? Praise be to God for the gift of His Son!"*

This is gross error! When I wrote Brother Reagan a letter questioning the truth of these statements, his response to me was that if I did not believe this, *"then you do not know the Jesus of the Bible."* And there is more.

Charles Swindoll says:

> *"That infant flesh so fair housed the Almighty God. Do you see the child and the glory, the infant-God? What you are seeing is the Incarnation -* **God dressed in diapers***" (Jesus: When God Became A Man; p. 4-5).*

Max Lucado writes in error:

> *"Angels watched as* **Mary changed God's diaper.** *The universe watched with wonder as* **the Almighty learned to walk***" (Max Lucado; God Came Near; p. 26).*

Respected Christian author Philip Yancey says:

> *"Unimaginably the* **Maker** *of all things* **shrank down, down, down,** *so small as to become an ovum, a single fertilized egg that would divide and re-divide until a fetus took shape, enlarging cell by cell inside a nervous teenager. The* **God** *who roared...***this God** *emerged in Palestine as a*

252

> baby **who could not speak or eat solid food or control his bladder**" *(The Jesus I Never Knew; p. 36).*

Writer C.S. Lewis said of the Incarnation:

> *"The Eternal Being, became a fetus inside a woman's body. If you want to get the hang of it, think how you would like to **become a slug or a crab**" (Mere Christianity; p. 155).*

I love these men but the degree of Christian blindness betrayed by these ridiculous statements is shocking! So what does the Bible really teach regarding the birth of Jesus?

- Nine hundred years before the birth of God's human Son, God was anticipating his future arrival:

  > *"**I will** be his father, and he **shall** be my son"* (2 Samuel 7:14; Heb. 1:5). Notice the future tense, so this was not from eternity past. *See also* Psalm 2:7, *"Thou art my Son; **this day** have I begotten thee."*

- Seven hundred years before Jesus' birth, the prophet Isaiah pictured a miraculous *conception*, and not an incarnation:

  > *"Behold, a virgin shall **conceive**, and bear a son..." (Isaiah 7:14).*

- The angel Gabriel spoke to Joseph regarding the virgin Mary and said:

  *"...that which is **conceived** in her is of the Holy Ghost" (Matt. 1:20).*

- Gabriel said to Mary:

  *"And, behold, thou shalt **conceive** in thy womb, and bring forth a son, and shall call his name Jesus. And, behold, thy cousin Elisabeth, she hath **also conceived a son**..."(Luke 1:31, 36).*
  Note: I know who the mother of the biblical Jesus is, but who is the mother of this *"eternal Son"* Jesus that Christianity teaches in error?

- Mary and Joseph brought the baby Jesus *"to Jerusalem, to present him to The Lord" (Luke 2:22)*, and they called him *"Jesus, which was so named of the angel before he was **conceived** in the womb" (v. 21).*

Question. Does God know the difference between a *conception* and an *incarnation*? It is for sure that He does! So we must conclude from His word that Mary's womb provided whatever a mother provides in childbirth, and the Spirit of God through a creative act, provided whatever a father provides, to produce **a real human baby**, who would become *"the man Christ Jesus" (I Tim. 2:5)*. With the Holy Bible stating at least these four times that Jesus' birth was by a **miraculous conception**, what spirit is behind this age-old attempt to make it an Incarnation?

Listen to Jesus!

> *"But now ye seek to kill me, **a man** [Greek-anthropos-Strong's #444-"a human being"] that hath told you the truth, which I have heard of God..." (John 8:40).* Here is one of Jesus' many claims to **manhood**, now where is his claim to **Godhood**?

What must we believe about Jesus in order to be saved?

Since this book is a prayerful search for the truth regarding "God and Jesus," we should consider the following question: According to Holy Scripture, what belief about Jesus is required for salvation?

Listen to Simon Peter:

> *"Thou art the Christ* [Messiah], *the **Son** of the living God" (Matt. 16:16).* Note: Not *"the living God,"* but *"the **Son** of the living God!"*

Listen to the apostle John as to why he wrote his Gospel:

> *"But these* [truths] *are written, that ye might believe that Jesus is the Christ* [Messiah] *the **Son** of God; and that **believing** ye might have life through his name" (John 20:31).* Again, not *"God,"* but, *"Messiah, the **Son** of God!"*

255

Listen to the eunuch's confession before water baptism by Philip:

> *"I **believe** that Jesus Christ is **the Son of God**"*
> *(Acts 8:37).*

Listen to Paul's first sermon after his Damascus road encounter with Jesus:

> *"And straightway he preached Christ in the synagogues, that he is **the Son of God**" (Acts 9:20).*

Listen to Jesus' declaration made some 60 years after his ascension to the Father:

> *"These things saith **the Son of God**" (Rev. 2:18).*
> Notice carefully: Not *"God,"* or *"God the Son!"*

In John 20:31 above, God through the apostle, makes an awesome promise to those who believe that *"**Jesus is the Messiah, the Son of God.**"* That promise is eternal *"life!"* He continues that thought in his epistle called I John.

> *"Whosoever shall **confess** that Jesus is **the Son of God, God dwelleth in him**, and he in God" (I John 4:15).*

> *"Whosoever **believeth** that **Jesus is the Messiah** is **born of God**" (I John 5:1).*

> *"Who is **he that overcometh the world**, but he*
> *that **believeth** that Jesus is **the Son of God**" (I*
> *John 5:5).*

> *"...that ye may know that ye have **eternal life**,*
> *and that ye may **believe** on the name of **the Son***
> ***of God**" (I John 5:13).*

These are some of God's unfailing promises to those who believe that Jesus is the **Messiah, the Son of God**. Question: Where are the promises made to those who believe that Jesus is *"God," "God the Son,"* or *"the second person of the Trinity?"* **They cannot be found!**

As incredible as it may seem, every person who says that Jesus is the "Son of God" is saying that he is not God, because he cannot be both God, and the Son of God. Furthermore, every person who says Jesus died on the cross is saying that he is not God, because God cannot die, He is "immortal" (i.e. incapable of dying) (I Timothy 1:17, etc.). Ten thousand atomic bombs could not kill God!

Wasted Worship!

The issues we are dealing with in this book could not be more serious or more worthy of our prayerful study, since they pertain not only to our knowledge of who the One Most High God is, but also to the worship we offer to Him. Jesus said that those who worship God, **must worship Him** *"in truth"* (John 4:24). That means the *"truth"* regarding who He alone **is**, and what He alone has **done**. Notice Jesus' forceful word "must". Then what happens to *worship* that is not based on the truth regarding God? Is it wasted? Likely! In Mark chapter seven, Jesus quoted God, speaking through the prophet Isaiah to Israel:

> *"Howbeit **in vain** do they worship me, teaching for doctrines the commandments of men. For laying aside the **commandment of God**, ye hold the tradition of men..." (Mark 7:7, 8).*

Wow! It was Jesus who told the inquirer in Mark 12:29 that **God's greatest commandment** is: *"Listen, O Israel; The Lord our **God is one Lord**."* What? *"God is **one** Lord!"* That is the message of the Bible from front to back but Christianity has followed the teachings of blind guides, calling it "Church tradition", and fallen into a ditch of confusion as to who God is. The truth is so simple, and to honest hearted people, has such a familiar ring to it. Why? Because Paul taught that God has written the truth regarding Himself in every heart *(Rom. 1:19,20; 2:14,15).* Tradition has written the doctrines of the Incarnation and the Trinity in people's *minds*, but God has never written these errors in their *hearts*! Now look at Jesus' words in Mark 7:9:

> *"And he said unto them, Full well ye reject the commandment of God, that ye might keep your own **tradition**."*

And was their worship of God accepted! Notice:

> *"Howbeit **in vain** do they worship me... ."*

Here are two questions for your consideration.

• Does God reach out and take the worship that is given to Mary, and claim it as His own? I think not!

• Does God reach out and take the worship that is given to *"the man Christ Jesus,"* as "Almighty God," "King of heaven", "God incarnate", and claim it for Himself? I am afraid not!

What Jesus taught regarding worship

According to Scripture, Jesus only mentioned *"worship"* on four occasions during his earthly ministry. They are:

1. When he refused to worship Satan, saying: *"...It is written, Thou shalt worship the **Lord thy God**..." (Matt. 4:10; Luke 4:8).*

2. When he quoted **God** saying through Isaiah: *"Howbeit in vain do they worship **me**..." (Mark 7:7).*

3. When he said to the woman at the well: *"the true worshipers shall worship the **Father**..." (John 4:23).*

4. When he said regarding a guest who is invited to a wedding, takes the lowest seat and is then given a higher seat: *"then shalt **thou have worship** in the presence of them that sit at meat with thee" (Luke 14:10).*

In the verse above Jesus introduces into his teaching the idea of *secondary worship.* This is not *God worship* but *"glory"* (Greek - *doxa* - *Strongs #1391*) which in broad application means *"dignity, honor, praise, worship."* Jesus said **ordinary people** can have this type of *"worship."* After he has been in heaven with the Father for some sixty years he again speaks of *secondary worship.* He says to overcoming saints in Revelation 3:9, regarding their enemies:

> *"...behold, I will make them to come and **worship before thy feet**, and to know that I have loved thee."*

The word *"worship"* in the verse above is the Greek word *"proskuneo" (Strongs #4352)* and it means *"to prostrate oneself in homage (do reverence to, adore): worship."* This is the same word used thirteen times **for the *"worship"* that was given to Jesus while he was on earth.** Of course he was worshiped as Messiah, virgin-born Son of God, which is far higher *worship* than any other man could ever receive, but his worship is still not *"God worship,"* but *"secondary worship."* Notice:

> *"Where is he that is born King of the Jews? For we have seen his star in the east, and are come to worship* [Gk. proskuneo] *him"* (Matt. 2:2). Note: Not *"God,"* but the *"King of the Jews."*

> *"Then came to him the mother of Zebedee's children with her sons, worshiping* [proskuneo] *him, and desiring a certain thing of him"* (Matt. 20:20). Note: This mother did not think she was worshiping *"God,"* since Jesus did not even have the authority to say who would sit on his right and left hands in his own kingdom (*"is not mine to give"* v. 23).

Secondary worship in the Old Testament

> *"And all the congregation blessed the **Lord God**
> of their fathers, and bowed down their heads,
> and worshiped the Lord* [God], **and the king**
> [Solomon]*" (I Chron. 29:20).*

The reason it is so important to understand the concept of *secondary worship* in the Bible, is that, in Christian pulpits it is often said that since Jesus received *"worship"* during his ministry, *"he must be God."* This is absolutely false, since we have shown in the preceding verses that people of God sometime receive *"worship"* with His approval. But to worship any person as *"God,"* except the **Lord God** Himself, is to flirt with idolatry!

> *"I am the **Lord thy God**, which have brought
> thee out of the Land of Egypt... . **Thou shalt
> have no other gods before me**"* [the **Lord God**
> speaking] *(Ex. 20:2-3).*

> *"Get thee behind me, Satan: for it is written,
> Thou shalt worship the **Lord thy God**, and **him
> only** shalt thou serve"* [Jesus Christ speaking]
> *(Matt. 4:10; Luke 4:8).* Note: After making
> such a statement, Jesus for sure never sought
> **God the Father's worship** for himself!

An exclusive word

It is important to note that there is one Greek word in the New Testament manuscripts that is translated *"worship,"* which is never

ever given to anyone but the one **Lord God**. It is the Greek word *"latreuo"* and it means *"to minister (to God), i.e. render religious homage - worship."* This word is reserved for **God** alone.

> *"...so* **worship** [latreuo] *I the* **God** *of my fathers"* [Paul speaking] *(Acts 24:14).*

> *"For we are the circumcision, which* **worship** [latreuo] ***God*** *in the spirit, and rejoice in Christ Jesus..." (Phil. 3:3).* Notice: We *"rejoice in Christ Jesus"* **but,** we *"worship God."*

Eleven N.T. references to worshiping "God." Question. Where are the verses that say, *"worship Jesus?"*

1. **Matt. 4:10** *"Then saith Jesus unto him, Get thee hence, Satan: for it is written, Thou shalt* **worship** *the Lord thy* **God***, and* **him only** *shalt thou serve."*

2. **Luke 4:8** *"Get thee behind me, Satan: for it is written, Thou shalt* **worship** *the Lord thy* **God***, and* **him only** *shalt thou serve."*

3. **John 4:24** *"**God** is a Spirit: and they that* **worship him** *must* **worship him** *in spirit and in truth."*

4. **Acts 18:13** *"Saying, This fellow persuadeth men to* **worship God**... ."*

5. **Acts 24:14** *"...so* **worship** *I the* **God** *of my fathers... ."*

6. **I Cor. 14:25** *"...and so falling down on his face he will **worship God**, and report that **God** is in you of a truth."*

7. **Phil. 3:3** *"For we...**worship God** in the spirit, and rejoice in Christ Jesus, and have no confidence in the flesh."*

8. **Rev. 11:1** *"Rise, and measure the temple of **God**, and the altar, and them that **worship** therein."*

9. **Rev. 14:7** *"Saying with a loud voice, Fear **God** and give glory to him...and **worship him** that made heaven, and earth, and the sea, and the fountains of waters."*

10. **Rev. 19:10** *"And I fell at his feet to worship him* [the angel]. *And he said unto me, See thou do it not: I am thy fellowservant, and of thy brethren that have the testimony of Jesus: **worship God**."* Notice: We *"have the testimony of Jesus"* but we are not told to worship him. We *"**worship God**."*

11. **Rev. 22:9** *"Then saith he unto me...**worship God**."*

What Paul believed regarding Christian worship and prayer

Paul's view of proper Christian worship is clearly seen in the following verses written to two N.T. churches:

> *"Speaking to yourselves in **psalms** and **hymns** and **spiritual songs**, singing and making melody in your heart to the Lord* [God]*; Giving thanks **always** for **all things** unto **God and the Father** in the name of our Lord Jesus Christ" (Eph. 5:19-20).* Question. Is this a picture of the worship in your church? Again Paul says:

> *"Let the word of Christ dwell in you richly as you teach and admonish one another with all wisdom, and as you sing **psalms, hymns** and **spiritual songs** with gratitude in your hearts **to God**. And whatever you do, whether in word or deed, do it all in the name of the Lord Jesus, giving thanks **to God the Father** through him" (Col. 3:16-17 NIV; NASB; NCV; Holman CSB; and The New English Bible).*

> *"For this cause **I bow my knees unto the Father** of our Lord Jesus Christ" (Eph. 3:14).*

> *"That ye may with **one mind** and **one mouth** glorify **God, even the Father** of our Lord Jesus Christ" (Romans 15:6).*

> *"For we are the circumcision, which **worship God** in the spirit, and **rejoice in Christ Jesus**,*

> *and have no confidence in the flesh" (Philippians*
> *3:3).*

What? "We rejoice in Christ Jesus", but no mention is made of worshiping him. We "worship God"! Here are some important facts for your consideration regarding this worship issue.

- The word "worship" is not used once regarding Jesus after his ascension to heaven.

- On four occasions in the book of Revelation, both God and the Lamb are present, but only **God** is "worshiped". They are Revelation 5:14 (see 4:11); 7:11; 11:15-17; and 19:4. Please study these verses carefully as this is very important to our understanding of "true" worship! Note: **They were worshiping God in the presence of Jesus**.

- The word Hallelujah (or Alleluia) is never spoken to Jesus in Scripture. It means *"praise to God"* and in the Bible is only given to The Lord God his Father. Note: Preachers who shout "Hallelujah to the Lamb of God," are betraying a serious lack of understanding as to who "God" and the "Lamb" are. *(See Rev. 19:1-6, 10 KJV; Psalm 146-150-God's Word Translation,* etc.).

- The phrases "praise Jesus" or "praising Jesus" cannot be found in Scripture. "Praise God" and "praising God" are found there many times! *(See Luke 1:64; 2:13, 20; 19:37; 24:53; Acts*

1:64; 2:47; 3:8,9; 16:25; Rev. 19:5, etc.). Why? Because Jesus says in John 5:41, ***"I do not accept praise from men"*** *(NIV).* Then why is Christianity so determined to "give all the praise to Jesus"? (I take it for granted dear reader that you do want the truth).

Worship the God of Jesus

Jesus has a God *whom he worships (Ps. 18:49; John 4:22-23), whom he fears (Isa. 11:1-5; Heb. 5:7); and to whom he prays (Matt. 26:53; Luke 6:12, 22:44; Heb. 7:25).* Notice these Scriptures regarding Jesus and **his God**.

> *"He shall stand and feed in the strength of the Lord, in the majesty of the name of **the Lord his God**" (Micah 5:4).*

> *"**My God, my God,** why hast thou forsaken me?" (Matt. 27:46).*

> *"...I am not yet ascended to my Father: but go to my brethren, and say unto them, I ascend unto my Father, and your Father: **and to my God, and your God**" (John 20:17).* Jesus is saying in essence, *"your God is my God."*

> *"The **God** and Father of our Lord Jesus Christ, which is blessed for evermore..." (II Cor. 11:31).*

> *"Blessed be the **God** and Father of our Lord Jesus Christ" (Eph. 1:3).*

266

> *"That the **God** of our Lord Jesus Christ, the Father of glory may give unto you the spirit of wisdom and revelation in the knowledge of **him**"* *(Eph. 1:17).*

> *"Blessed be the **God** and Father of our Lord Jesus Christ" (I Peter 1:3).*

> *"He that overcometh will I make a pillar in the temple of **my God**...name of **my God**...city of **my God**...down out of heaven from **my God**" (Rev. 3:12).*

My friend, after seeing the overwhelming evidence set forth in this book regarding God and Jesus, an important decision must be made. Will you give your worship to Jesus Messiah, or will you worship the **God** of Jesus?

The danger of Christian idolatry

Professor James D.G. Dunn, one of the most noted **trinitarian** scholars in the world, has written a book titled, *Did The First Christians Worship Jesus?* In the final chapter he states some shocking conclusions:

> *"One is that there are some problems, even **dangers**, in Christian worship if it is defined too simply as worship of Jesus. For...it soon becomes evident that Christian worship can deteriorate into what may be called **Jesus-olatry**.*

*That is, not simply into worship of Jesus, but into a worship that falls short of **the worship due to the one God and Father** of our Lord Jesus Christ. I used the term **'Jesus-olatry'** as in an important sense parallel or even **close to** 'idolatry.' As Israel's prophets pointed out on several occasions, the calamity of idolatry is that the idol is in effect taken to be the god to be worshipped. The **danger of Jesus-olatry** is similar: **that Jesus has been substituted for God, has taken the place of the one creator God; Jesus is absorbing the worship due to God alone.** So the **danger** with a worship that has become too predominantly the worship of Jesus is that **the worship due to God is stopping at Jesus,** and that the revelation of God through Jesus and **the worship of God through Jesus** is being stifled and short-circuited. It was because of such concerns that one of the leading figures and theologians of the early charismatic movement in the UK wrote a book entitled, The Forgotten **Father. His warning still needs to be heeded."***

To this I give a hearty "Amen!" Make no mistake about it, I love my Christian family. However, I must say in all sincerity that Christianity reminds me of a pitiful little kid following his older brother around, thinking he is his daddy. Thank God for the brother, but someone needs to introduce this child to his father! If

268

you do not know who your Father is, then you don't know who you are in Him!

But we will get it right. The apostle John saw a mighty angel fly in the midst of heaven at the **time of the end**, having the **eternal gospel** to preach unto the **entire world** *(Rev. 14:6-7)*. The angel was...

> *"Saying with a loud voice, **Fear God**, and **give glory to him**...and **worship him** that made heaven, and earth, and the sea, and the fountains of waters."*

This is **fear, glory, and worship to God our Creator** in the name of our savior Jesus Messiah. That is the message of this book which cannot be biblically refuted!*

In Christian Love,
Joel Hemphill

*For further understanding of this awesome subject let the Holy Spirit guide you as you read the Bible. Also, may I recommend my books *"To God Be The Glory,"* and *"Glory To God In The Highest,"* available from Trumpet Call Books, wherever fine books are sold.

Paul's View Of True Christian Worship

*"Speaking to yourselves in psalms and hymns and spiritual songs, singing and making melody in your heart to the Lord; Giving thanks **always** for **all things** unto **God and the Father** in the name of our Lord Jesus Christ"(Eph. 5:19-20).*

*"Let the word of Christ dwell in you richly as you teach and admonish one another with all wisdom, and as you sing psalms, hymns and spiritual songs with gratitude in your hearts **to God**. And whatever you do, whether in word or deed, do it all in the name of the Lord Jesus, **giving thanks to God the Father** through him" (Col. 3:16-17).*

*"For this cause I bow my knees **unto the Father** of our Lord Jesus Christ" (Ephesians 3:14).*

*"That ye may with one mind and one mouth **glorify God, even the Father** of our Lord Jesus Christ" (Romans 15:6).*

Appendix A

Learning About God From Jesus

*T*he following is a summary of what Jesus' words and actions teach us regarding the identity of God.

If Mary and Joseph took the baby Jesus to the temple *"to present him **to the Lord** [God],"* then he himself cannot be God *(Luke 2:22)*.

If Jesus as a boy *"**increased**...in favor with **God**,"* then he cannot be God *(Luke 2:52)*.

If Jesus said his Father is *"the **only** true God"* then he himself cannot be God. *(John 17:3)*.

If Jesus said *"Why callest thou me good, there is none good but **one**, that is God,"* he cannot be God *(Matt. 19:17)*.

If Jesus said *"I can of mine own self do nothing...If I bear witness of myself, my witness is not true,"* then he cannot be God *(John 5:30-31)*.

If Jesus said *"my Father is greater than I,"* he cannot be God, because none can be *"greater"* than God *(John 14:28)*.

If Jesus said *"I...am set down with my Father in **his throne"*** then he cannot be God *(Rev. 3:21)*.

If Jesus said, when Lazarus died in Bethany *"I was not there,"* then he cannot be God, for God is omnipresent *(John 11:15)*.

If Jesus claimed the Father as *"my God"* seven times in the N.T., he himself cannot be God *(Matt. 27:46; John 20:17; Rev. 3:12)*.

If Jesus claimed to be a *"man"* (Greek - anthropos *"a human being"*), again and again in Scripture, he cannot be God *(John 8:28, 40; 12:23)*.

If Jesus was *"driven by the Spirit into the wilderness"* and was *"forty days, **tempted** of Satan" (Mark 1:12-13)*, then he cannot be God, for *"God cannot be tempted" (James 1:13)*.

If Jesus went to his home town of Nazareth *"and he could there do no mighty work"* because of their unbelief, he cannot be God *(Mark 6:5-6)*.

If Jesus went to a fig tree seeing leaves, but not knowing if it had figs, then he cannot be God because God knows **all** *(Mark 11:13)*.

If Jesus did not have the authority to decide who would sit on his right or left hand **in his own kingdom,** and said it *"is not mine to give,"* then he cannot be God *(Matt. 20:23)*.

If Jesus did not have *"the times or the seasons"* in his power, then he cannot be God *(Acts 1:7)*.

If Jesus left planet earth to go to the Father, not knowing when he would return, then he cannot be God *(Matt. 24:36; Mark 13:32)*.

If Jesus did not know the end-time events as recorded in *Revelation*, until after he ascended to the Father and **God revealed them to him,** then he cannot be God *(Rev. 1:1)*.

Every Christian that says Jesus died on the cross, is saying he is not God because **God cannot die!** God is *"immortal"* which means *"deathless, incapable of dying."* Jesus was mortal, *"appointed to death" (Heb. 9:27-28)*. Ten thousand atomic bombs could not kill God!

If the disciples who saw Jesus ascend to heaven in Acts chapter one, **did not pray to him in Acts chapter four,** then he cannot be God *(Acts 4:24-30)*.

If Jesus said *"I am the vine, ye are the branches"* and *"my Father is the husbandman"* [i.e. the farmer, owner of the vineyard], then he himself cannot be God *(John 15:1, 5)*.

If Jesus referred to himself as the *"Amen, the faithful and true witness, **the beginning of the creation of God,**"* then he cannot be God *(Rev. 3:14)*.

*"We know what **we** worship"* [Jesus speaking] *(John 4:22)*. Jesus joins us in worshiping *"the only true God,"* **his God** and **our God**.

*"...The testimony of Jesus: **Worship God**" (Rev. 19:10)*.

*"...**Worship God**" (Rev. 22:9)*.

Non-biblical Terminology

The following terms used frequently in teaching the doctrines of the "Oneness" and "Trinity" are not biblical terminology.

Trinity	Triune	Triad
Blessed Trinity	Holy Trinity	God the Son
2nd person of the Trinity	3rd person of the Trinity	1st person of the Trinity
God the Holy Spirit	The eternal Son of God	Eternally begotten
God incarnate	God in flesh	Incarnation
God-man	Dual nature	Double nature
Two natures	Jehovah Jesus	Very God and very man
Fully God and fully man	Eternally proceeding	The diety of Christ

There is not one verse of Scripture that says that God is "three" of anything! Not:

Three co-equal, co-eternal persons	Three persons of one essence
One God in three persons	Three essences of one person
Three persons of God	God in three persons
Eternal three	Three in one God
Three Gods	Three Spirits
Three divinities	Three persons
Three modes	Three beings
Three substances	Three agents
Three attributes	Three offices
Three entities	Three infinite minds

Appendix B

A Unique Sinless Man

*J*esus Christ is the supernaturally conceived, virgin born, sinless Son of God. He is the perfect man, unique man, the mirror image of God, *"the express **image** of His person" (Heb. 1:3),* but **man nevertheless**. *"One mediator between God and men, **the man** Christ Jesus" (I Tim. 2:5)*

Jesus himself said so:
*   *"And no **man** hath ascended up to heaven, but he that came down from heaven..." (John 3:13).*
*   *"But now ye seek to kill me, **a man** that has told you the truth, **which I have heard of God**" (John 8:40).*
*   *"Greater love hath no **man** than this, that **a man** lay down his life for his friends. Ye are my friends..." (John 15:13-14).*
*   *"If I had not done among them the works which **none other man** did, they had not had sin" (John 15:24).* Please note: Jesus never once in Scripture said he is God, but these three times he clearly referred to himself as a **man**.

The Old Testament prophets said so:
*   *"**A man** of sorrows and acquainted with grief" (Isa. 53:3).*
*   *"David shall never want **a man** to sit upon the throne of the house of Israel" (Jer. 33:17).*
*   *"Awake, O sword against **the man** that is my fellow" (Zech. 13:7; Matt. 26:31).*
*   *"And **this man** shall be the peace" (Micah 5:5)*

John the Baptist said so:

- *"After me cometh **a man** who is preferred before me"* *(John 1:30)*.
- *"All things that John spoke of **this man** were true"* *(John 10:41)*.

The apostle Paul said so:

- *"Through **this man** is preached unto you the forgiveness of sins"* *(Acts 13:38)*.
- "[God] *will judge the world...by **that man** whom he hath ordained"* *(Acts 17:31)*.
- *"The gift of grace, which is by **one man**, Jesus Christ"* *(Rom. 5:15)*.
- *"**Every man** in his own order: Christ the firstfruits"* [in resurrection] *(I Cor. 15:23)*.
- *"And being found in fashion as **a man**"* *(Phil. 2:8)*.
- *"Put on the **new man**"* [Christ] *(Col. 3:10)*.
- *"For there is **one God**, and one mediator between God and men, **the man Christ Jesus**"* *(I Tim. 2:5)*.

The writer of Hebrews said so:

- *"For **this man** was counted worthy of more glory than Moses"* *(Heb. 3:3)*.
- *"But **this man**...hath an unchangeable priesthood"* *(Heb. 7:24)*.
- *"It is of necessity that **this man** have somewhat to offer"* *(Heb. 8:3)*.
- *"But **this man**...sat down on the right hand of God"* *(Heb. 10:12)*.

Jesus is the last Adam, not the first God-man. Listen to the apostle Paul:

- *"For since **by man came death, by man came also** the resurrection of the dead. For as in **Adam** all die, even so in **Christ** shall all be made alive"* (I Cor. 15:21-22).

- *"The **first man Adam** was made a living soul: the **last Adam** was made a quickening spirit"* (I Cor. 15:45). *"The **first man**...the **second man**"* (v. 47).

Jesus as *"the **last Adam**"* was genetically equal to the *"**first man Adam**."* Adam was created by God from the dust in Genesis one. Jesus was created by God (the Holy Ghost) in the womb of the virgin Mary in Matthew one and Luke one *(Matt. 1:20; Luke 1:32, Rev. 3:14; Col. 1:15 & 3:10)*. Study carefully Galatians 4:4:

> *"But when the fulness of the time was come, God sent forth his Son, **made of a woman, made** under the law."* The word *"made"* is *"ginomaï"* in Greek and means *"to generate - cause to come into being"*. This was a **creative act** of the Holy Spirit and not an incarnation.

Jesus is a glorified man at the right hand of God

- *"Jesus of Nazareth, **a man** approved of God"* [Peter speaking of the ascended Jesus, at Pentecost] *(Acts 2:22)*.

- *"Behold, I see the heavens opened and **the Son of man** standing on the right hand of God"* [Stephen] *(Acts 7:56)*.

- *"But **this man**, after he had offered one sacrifice for sins for ever, sat down on the **right hand of God"** (Heb. 10:12)*.

<u>Note:</u> Jesus referred to himself as *"Son of **man**"* over 80 times in the Gospels and it means *"a human being."* The phrase comes from Psalms 8:6 according to Hebrews 2:6. God called Ezekiel *"son of man"* 90 times in the book of Ezekiel. Whatever Ezekiel was as to manhood, Jesus was. Jesus came as a human being. He had a human body, mind, spirit, soul, will and personality. The *"first Adam"* was made with a sinless nature, but as an act of his will he sinned anyway. The *"last Adam"* was made sinless, with blood untainted by the sin of the first Adam, and as an act of his will he *"did no sin, neither was guile found in his mouth"* (I Peter 2:22). He did it, not as a God-man, but as **a man**. Jesus *"condemned sin in the flesh" (Rom. 8:3)*! *"**Wherefore** God also hath highly exalted him" (Phil. 2:9).*

Consider This!

*"From the middle of the 2nd century A.D., **Christians** who had some training in **Greek philosophy** began to feel the need to express their faith in **its terms**... The philosophy that suited them best was **Platonism**. The first Christian to use **Greek philosophy** in the service of the Christian faith was Justin Martyr. Each of the great **Christian Platonists** understood Platonism and applied it to the understanding of his faith in his own individual way. But the **Christian Platonism** that had the widest, deepest, and most lasting influence in the West was that of St. Augustine of Hippo. In his theology, insofar as Augustine's thought about God was **Platonic**, he conformed fairly closely to the general pattern of Christian Platonism... .*

***Perhaps the most distinctive influence of Plotinian Neo-Platonism on Augustine's thinking about God** was in his **Trinitarian theology**. Because he thought that something like the **Christian doctrine of the Trinity** was to be found in Plotinus and Porphyry [two followers of Plato], he tended to regard it as a **philosophical doctrine** and tried to make philosophical sense of it... ."*

(Britannica - Macropaedia; Vol. 25; p. 903-904

This large painting by Raphael (circa 1509) is titled, **The School of Athens**, and is in the Vatican's Apostolic Palace. It depicts Socrates (1), Plato (2), Aristotle (3), and other Greek philosophers (Heraclitus - Zeno - Boethius, etc.) who greatly influenced trinitarian Christian doctrine. "The building is in the shape of a Greek cross...to show a harmony between pagan philosophy and Christian theology."

Socrates

These marble busts of **Socrates** and **Plato** have places of honor in the Vatican in recognition of their contributions to Christian theology (its doctrine of God.)

282

About The Author

Joel Hemphill.....

Has been married to his wife LaBreeska for fifty-six years.

Has been a minister of Jesus Christ for over fifty years.

Has written and recorded over 300 Gospel songs. Along with his family has received eight Dove Awards, and has received ten Dove nominations as Song Writer of the Year.

Has been inducted into the Southern Gospel Music Hall of Fame, the Southern Songwriters Hall of Fame, and the State of Louisiana's Delta Music Hall of Fame and Museum.

Has ministered in Israel, Egypt, South Africa, the U.K., Germany, Austria, Honduras and throughout North America.
Received a revelation in Holy Scripture in 2005 regarding the One Most High God, and has written revolutionary books on this subject, including *"To God Be The Glory,"* and *"Glory To God In The Highest."*

Through his books, CDs, website and seminars is helping ministers of various denominations come to this biblical understanding.

NOTES

For Music & Preaching CDs, Prayer,
Books by Joel & LaBreeska
or additional copies of this book
please write or phone:

Joel & LaBreeska Hemphill
P.O. Box 656
Joelton, Tennessee 37080
Phone: 615/299-0848
Fax: 615/299-0849

email: jhemphill@wildblue.net

www.thehemphills.com
www.trumpetcallbooks.com

**To hear Joel teach 7 lessons on the awesome subject
of the One Most High God
go to www.trumpetcallbooks.com**

A Reward Is Offered!

According to Holy Scripture, Jesus of Nazareth is the supernaturally conceived, virgin-born, sinless, human Son of God; savior, redeemer, Messiah, future ruler of this planet for the coming 1000 years, and the only way to God!

In support of that truth I offer a $10,000.00 reward for any verse in the KJV Bible where Jesus claimed to be "God", "God the Son", or made one statement regarding a "Trinity".

Since Jesus Christ, the founder of the Christian religion never said these things, I advise my Christian family to stop saying them!

Joel Hemphill

CPSIA information can be obtained at www.ICGtesting.com
Printed in the USA
LVOW02s0751110813

346666LV00001BA/1/P